HEART OF A SCOUNDREL

"Unhand me, sir!" Katherine trembled with rage.

"Are we not kissing cousins, then?" he asked, still retaining his hold.

"No, we are not, as you very well know!" she hissed.

He leaned down again, ignoring her panic, and whispered, "You will bring about the very thing you fear if you are not quiet. You must pretend at all times that I am James Daniel St. Cloud. It is the only way to succeed."

Katherine recognized the wisdom of his words, but his closeness disturbed her. "Release me, please."

"As soon as you promise to abide by my words, bonny Kate."

"I will not speak of this again," she grated. "And do not call me Kate! That is common!"

Daniel smiled. "You could never be considered common, Katherine."

MOONLIGHT CHARADE

JUDITH CHRISTENBERRY

JOVE BOOKS, NEW YORK

MOONLIGHT CHARADE

A Jove Book / published by arrangement with
the author

PRINTING HISTORY
Jove edition / February 1991

ISBN: 0-515-10492-2

Jove Books are published by The Berkley Publishing Group,
200 Madison Avenue, New York, New York 10016.
The name "JOVE" and the "J" logo
are trademarks belonging to Jove Publications, Inc.

PRINTED IN THE UNITED STATES OF AMERICA

10 9 8 7 6 5 4 3 2 1

MOONLIGHT CHARADE

Prologue

"Miss Katherine."

A voice hissed across the quiet afternoon, startling the young woman who was striding toward the large mansion sitting regally on top of the hill. Her blue velvet riding habit was the height of fashion, but the mud splattered on its skirt did not denote a genteel ride. The subject that dominated her thoughts was not genteel either. She was debating the merits of planting oats or hay in the east meadow.

"Miss Katherine," the voice called again, this time louder, and she turned toward a tree only a few yards distant from the well-trimmed path to the big house. "Jacob? Is that you?"

The small, dapper figure of her father's valet peeked out at her. "Yes, miss. But I mustn't be seen. I'm supposed to be polishing the furniture in the Master's bedroom."

"What is it?" she asked, stepping closer to him.

"I've found him."

"What? My cousin is here?" Katherine shrieked before remembering to remain quiet.

"Course not. I mean I've found one who could . . . you know, like you asked."

"Are you sure?"

"He's the best as has come along these past weeks. And we only have one more week, you remember."

"I remember," Katherine said with a sigh. "Where is he?"

"He just arrived at the inn. I was having a pint when he got there."

"I thought you were supposed to be working here," Katherine teased.

"I'm a gentleman's gentleman, Miss Katherine. I'm not supposed to do the polishing!" the small man said indignantly.

"I know, Jacob. If our plan works, perhaps you will once again be able to do proper work. I'll go to the inn at once. How will I know—"

"His name is Hawthorne, and he's a big man."

"Big? You mean tall? Father was not exceptionally tall, but I suppose—"

"We've not got much time left. He's the best one. You must make do with 'im."

"All right, all right. I'll . . . I'll go."

Chapter One

The tall man surveyed the room assigned to him by the burly master of the Red Lion Inn. It was not elegant, but he had slept in worse places. Besides, his travels had made him weary. A knock on the door revealed a saucy young maid bearing the jug of warm water he had requested. In spite of her unspoken invitation, he took only the water and again closed the door. He needed a wash and a shave.

He had allowed his beard to grow on the trip across the ocean from Canada, but it was time to be clean-shaven again. Though he had not traveled with a valet, it was of no importance. He had learned to care for himself when he spent two winters in the mountains trapping beaver.

While he was finishing the job of removing his heavy beard, there was a second knock. He was not surprised to discover the maid at his door. Women were attracted to his broad-shouldered, muscular body and used the slightest of pretexts to offer themselves for his pleasure.

"Sorry, miss, but I'm tired."

With a twist of her shoulders, she replied, "And I'm not offerin', sir. There be a lady below to see you."

"To see me? I know no one here. You must be mistaken."

"I don't see how I could be, sir, since she asked for you by name."

With a frown, Daniel Hawthorne wiped his cheeks dry and tightened the lacing on his shirt, unmindful of the young woman's admiring look.

"Where down below?"

"She's in the private parlor, a course. After all, it's Miss Katherine come to call."

"You know her?"

"Well, a course I do. It's Miss Katherine St. Cloud, what lives in the big house on the cliff."

No emotion showed on the man's face now as he fixed his cuffs. "Thank you. Tell Miss St. Cloud I'll be down directly." He turned away to pick up a blue frock coat, out of style and slightly worn.

The maid paused in admiration before she scooted down the hall, aware of her employer's displeasure if she were caught loitering with the guests.

Katherine paced the private parlor, a nervous habit, and wondered for the thousandth time if she were doing the right thing. "It won't harm anyone," she argued aloud with herself. She had been having this discussion for a number of weeks, but she always arrived at the same conclusion. She had no choice. But her hands remained tightly clinched, hidden by the folds of her gray silk gown.

She whirled around as the door opened and almost cried out in disappointment. In the opening stood a large man, his form muscular and impressive. "You have black hair!"

The well-formed eyebrows raised, and Katherine was

close enough to see the twinkle in the blue eyes quite like her own.

"So I had thought, madam. Does it displease you?"

"Oh, no, no, of course not, but it would have been so much better had you been blond."

A smile was added to his expression as he said, "While I admire the beauty of your locks, young lady, there are those who do not despise my black hair."

Katherine had no difficulty accepting his statement as truth. The man was quite handsome, and she was sure many women were attracted to him. But that had nothing to do with her need.

"I apologize, sir, for my remarks. Allow me to introduce myself. I am Miss St. Cloud. I . . . I live near here." She faltered. "That is, I have need of . . . I would like to hire a man to . . . would you care to sit down?"

His imperturbable expression unnerved her, and she needed him seated so he would not tower over her.

"I had not realized manners were so different here."

"I beg your pardon?" she asked bewilderedly.

"In Canada, madam, although it is considered a heathenish country, gentlemen do not seat themselves in the presence of a lady who remains standing."

Katherine's face turned crimson, and she hurried to the sofa and sat down. "It is no different in England, sir, but I was concentrating on my speech."

He strolled leisurely to a nearby chair. He seemed elegant in spite of his rough clothing. "How may I serve you?"

Gratified, Katherine smiled for the first time, her dimples framing her soft lips, as she leaned toward him.

"Truly, I do need your help, sir, but I am willing to pay for your services. And it will not be a difficult duty. Quite pleasurable, really, if you would care to live in an elegant home, wear fine clothes, and find leisure your companion."

His expressionless stare mesmerized her, so much that Katherine actually jumped when he murmured, "Most interesting. I cannot imagine anyone turning down such a position. May I ask why you have chosen to offer it to me, a stranger?"

"Oh, it had to be a stranger. And in particular a stranger from the Colonies. You are from America, aren't you?"

"No."

Katherine's face fell. "Oh, no! Then you will not do."

"Surely a few miles does not matter that much," he murmured with a half smile.

"A few miles?" Katherine demanded in confusion.

"I am from Montreal, in Lower Canada."

"Oh, of course. And that is part of the British Empire," Katherine realized aloud.

"For more than half a century," the man drawled.

Katherine sat frowning as she considered his words. "Then . . . perhaps you will do after all."

"For what are you considering me?"

His manner disturbed Katherine, reminding her that she was offering a great deal to someone about whom she knew nothing. He could be a thief or . . . or a murderer. She flashed a frightened gaze at her guest before looking away.

"Now why would you be frightened?" he asked gently.

"I'm not. Do not be absurd."

"So what must I do to obtain this employment?"

"Why, nothing, sir. That is, no work would be required of you. You must only claim to be my cousin."

There was silence while the tall, dark man studied the young lady sitting demurely on the sofa, blond ringlets framing her delicate features. "I have no objection to being your cousin, madam, but I'm not sure anyone would believe such."

"They must!" Katherine said with great intensity. "It is our only hope."

"You are being threatened?"

"Yes, and will be thrown out of our home."

"Who would do such a thing?"

"The King, or rather, the Prince Regent."

"And just by claiming to be your cousin, I could save you from so powerful a person as the Prince Regent?" he asked doubtfully.

"Yes."

With a wry smile, he rose and strolled over to the window to stare out into the yard of the inn, watching the passing traffic in the small town. He turned back around, the young woman having remained silently seated on the sofa. "Pardon me, madam, but even in the New World— or perhaps I should say, especially in the New World— we know of the King's powers. After all, we are his subjects too."

"Yes, but it is true. Please, come be seated and I will explain."

He followed her plea and waited for her to speak.

"You see, several generations ago, my great-great-grandfather, Robert St. Cloud, served King Charles in routing the Puritans and returning him to his rightful throne. He was rewarded with five thousand acres of land and the title of baron. But there was a reservation in the grant that if he or any of his descendants should die without a male heir, everything would revert to the Crown."

"Your father has five thousand acres?"

"No. No, the original grant was divided between the eldest son and a second son, who received fifteen hundred acres and then sold them. He was a ne'er-do-well and Father always said. . : . Oh, that doesn't matter. Anyway, when my brother died—"

"When was that?"

"Last year at Waterloo. He—he was killed with a musket ball. After his death, Father had the best solicitors look at the papers, hoping to break the terms of the grant. But they could not. So he determined to locate his cousin, who he said would provide for us, should . . . should anything happen to him."

"Then what is the difficulty?"

She bit her lip and blinked before saying, "Father died unexpectedly in a hunting accident six months ago before his cousin could be found."

With a wry smile, Mr. Hawthorne said, "Let me guess. The cousin disappeared to America and has not been heard from since."

"Yes. Yes, that is exactly what has happened."

"How long ago did he depart?" he asked, his eyes never leaving his companion's face.

"A little over thirty years, sir."

With raised brows, the man said, "I hate to disappoint so lovely a lady, but not even for you can I impersonate a man in his . . . " He paused to calculate. "Early fifties?"

"No, I know," Katherine said with regret, ignoring the smile on her companion's face. "But, you see, we have thought up a very good story."

"Who else is involved in this offer?"

"Only my father's valet, Jacob."

"Ah. And what is your story?"

"You will be his son. You can say he has died and you are his only heir. In fact," she added enthusiastically, "it will work very well that you are from Canada instead of America. That will explain why it took so long for you to get here. See how simple it will be?"

"And how will I prove it?"

Katherine stared at him, her smile wiped from her face. "I . . . I thought to find someone who would resemble . . . I do not know. What would be acceptable? Please, help me. We cannot just accept such a fate without some effort. My mother is frail, and she loves her home very much."

"We would need papers."

"What kind of papers?"

"Letters, perhaps. A bible with the date of my birth."

"We can write some letters. Do you think we could find an old bible and . . . " Katherine offered eagerly.

"Just a moment. I have not said I would take this offer of employment," the man reminded her as he resumed his seat.

"But . . ."

"There are some questions to be answered."

"What?" she demanded, frowning.

"How long would I be required to remain?"

"Why—why would you want to leave?" Katherine asked, puzzled.

"I might wish to return to Canada."

"But of course you could return. I would be perfectly willing to handle the estate. As a matter of fact, I would be doing so anyway. After all, you know nothing about it." She noted a disturbing look in his eyes but chose to ignore it.

"And as your cousin, I am to provide a home for you and your mother?"

"Of course you would. That is the whole purpose."

"And if you marry?"

"I—I would expect a reasonable marriage portion, but it is unlikely I shall marry," Katherine assured him.

"Why? I see no reason for you to remain on the shelf."

His eyes roamed her person, leaving her with an uncomfortable feeling.

Her chin rose as she answered, "I prefer to remain at home and care for my mother."

"And if I choose to marry?"

Katherine blinked several times. Somewhere she had lost control of this interview, and she felt as if she were caught in the undertow of the tide. "I see no problem . . . she must be someone agreeable to—to our remaining on the estate. Because, of course, you . . . I will be your employer."

"And how much do you intend to pay me?"

Gulping, Katherine did some quick addition in her head before saying, "You will receive one thousand pounds a year, and your living expenses. A very generous offer, sir," she assured him stoutly.

"Quite generous," he agreed.

"Then you will do it? We must hurry. The deadline the solicitors have set is in one week."

"The Crown would move fast?"

"Yes, because Sir William Ralston has already made a most generous bid for our land. He has been trying to acquire it for several years, and even though he is only a baronet, he has powerful friends," she added bitterly.

"And your father would not sell?"

"Oh, he did not offer for the land. He offered for me and asked for the land adjoining his as my dowry."

"And you had no desire to be his wife?"

"No! He is . . . not agreeable."

"And you have no *tendre* for any other?" he persisted.

"No, but that has nothing to do with my proposal."

He smiled, but changed the subject. "Your mother approves of this havey-cavey scheme?"

"No! Oh, no, Mother would not approve at all. She is a saint!" Katherine said with a touch of despair.

"Unlike her daughter?"

Blushing, Katherine said, "I do not misbehave, normally, but I am desperate."

"Very well. I will come to your rescue, cousin," he said with a smile.

"Oh! Thank you, Mr. Hawthorne. I am so grateful. Now, we must make plans. First of all, you must change your name."

"Won't the inn keeper think it strange that I registered under the name of Hawthorne and now tell everyone I am St. Cloud?"

"But what can we do? My cousin would not be named Hawthorne."

The man thought for a minute before saying, "Let us say that my father died when I was young and my mother remarried. Being such an adorable child, my stepfather wanted to adopt me. So I took his name. I registered under that name instead of St. Cloud."

Katherine frowned. "I suppose it is acceptable . . . expect the part about your being adorable as a child," she added, her dimples flashing.

"Incredible."

"I beg your pardon? What is incredible?"

"Your dimples, love."

"What did you call me?" she demanded in a starchy voice.

"Are we not cousins? Surely you do not stand on such formality with your cousin?" Daniel Hawthorne asked with a slanted smile.

"We have not begun our playacting yet, sir."

"And I am to bow down and call you Miss St. Cloud when we do?"

"No, I did not mean that, but . . . I am called Katherine."

"Katherine? A lovely name."

Though her cheeks were rosy, Katherine ignored his compliment. "What is your Christian name?"

"Daniel."

She frowned and he asked, "What should I be called?"

"Father's cousin was named James."

"Then I shall be James Daniel St. Cloud, named after my father but called Daniel."

"I suppose that will do, though, of course, it will be Lord St. Cloud. You will be a baron now."

"Just how close a cousin am I?" he suddenly demanded.

"Why do you ask?" Katherine asked cautiously, her eyes trained on the man across from her.

"I am just curious, that is all."

"James St. Cloud was the grandson of my father's grandfather's brother," she explained.

"Ah. That will do," Daniel Hawthorne alias St. Cloud said with a satisfied nod, an amused smile playing about his lips.

"I don't understand."

"It is nothing," he assured her, leaning back in his chair. "Now, you must explain the family to me, so I will make no mistakes when the lawyers interview me."

"Oh, I will insist on being present to assist you," she assured him.

"I do not think they will allow it. Besides, it will draw their suspicion if I do not give them the answers myself."

"Very well. Shall you take notes?"

"I have a good memory."

His mocking grin did little to reassure her, but Katherine instructed her newfound cousin in the rudiments of the St. Cloud family history for the next hour. When she finally ran out of aunts and uncles, long dead, to enumerate, her throat was dry. "I long for some tea."

"Then I will have some served."

"No! We must not. That will draw attention to our meeting," Katherine explained, alarmed at such a thought.

"The chambermaid is already aware of it."

"I did not think of that!" Katherine gasped. "And Mr. Muncie greeted me as I came in. He will remember I asked him to send her up to you! Oh dear!"

Her anxious face drew his immediate concern. "Do not worry so. I take it you know Mr. Muncie well?"

"Of course. I have been coming to his inn for his wife's delicious scones ever since I learned to ride."

"Very well. I will ring for him. When he arrives, you will tell him your long-lost cousin has arrived."

"But how did I know you were here?"

"I wrote you a letter. And you did not tell anyone because you did not want to raise false hopes should I be an impostor."

"But we don't have any proof yet."

"Mr. Muncie will take your word for my identity, and by the time the lawyers arrive . . ." He paused to ask, "Tomorrow?" At her nod, he continued. "I will have some documents prepared."

"You will be able to do that?"

"Yes. I have several talents of which you are as yet unaware."

Again a shiver of fear caused Katherine to tremble. She truly knew nothing about the man before her, and yet she intended to take him into her home and claim him as her cousin.

Watching her closely, Mr. Hawthorne said, "Have you changed your mind, Katherine? It is not too late."

She stared at him intently before whispering, "Yes, it is too late. I must trust you to save us. It is the only way. And I am truly grateful, Mr. Hawthorne," she finished strongly.

"I will not betray your trust," he assured her solemnly. "But you must remember to call me Daniel."

With a deep breath, as if taking a vow, she nodded.

"Then I will ring for Mr. Muncie. Are you ready, cousin?"

"Yes, Daniel, I am ready. Please ring the bell for tea."

When the door opened several minutes later, the young lady rose from her seat to greet the entering innkeeper, excited joy on her face. "Mr. Muncie, you will never guess! This gentleman is my long-lost cousin, Daniel St. Cloud!"

Chapter Two

"Do sit down, Katherine. It is unladylike to stride about as you do." The swish of Katherine's gray silken skirt ceased as she seated herself on the blue damask sofa next to her mother. For once, the elegance of the Blue Salon failed to calm her.

"Sorry, Mama dear. It is just that I am anxious to be done with all this. I have been so worried. . . ."

"As I was, love. But Daniel has arrived, and we have no more worries." The fragile woman wrapped in numerous shawls smiled. "He's such a charming man."

"Yes, of course," Katherine responded, her eyes trained once more on the door, as if she could will her new cousin's appearance if she only concentrated.

"I see no reason for the solicitors taking so long. After all, if we were satisfied with Daniel's identity, who are they to question it?"

Katherine's smile broadened at her mother's naiveté. "Sir William is most anxious to buy our land. You may be sure his solicitor will press any advantage." Katherine turned back to the door, her anxiety heightened by her own words.

In spite of her anticipation, the opening of the door caused her to gasp. Greyson, their longtime butler, held it open for three somber gentlemen, followed by her newly discovered "cousin." Katherine's eyes flew to the tall man who answered her unspoken question with the merest wink of an eye.

"Lady St. Cloud," the shortest of the three black-coated men said with a grimace meant for a smile, "this young gentleman has satisfied us that he is in truth James Daniel St. Cloud, now Lord St. Cloud, the only remaining male heir to White Oaks. We are pleased to be able to inform you of such," he added pompously.

Katherine knew Mr. Petersham was pleased since he had been her father's solicitor and looked to continue his association with Daniel. The other two solicitors, however, representing the Crown and Sir William, did not appear ecstatic with the news. Katherine's gaze traveled on to Daniel Hawthorne. St. Cloud, she reminded herself. It would be best to forget everything prior to today. Daniel's ability to prevaricate impressed her, however. He must be a master at it to have convinced those two.

"Do sit down, gentlemen," Lady St. Cloud said, after commanding Katherine, who had jumped to her feet upon their entrance, to a chair with her eyes. "Greyson will arrive with the tea tray shortly. I'm sure all your inquiries must have left your throats quite dry."

Katherine requested Daniel's presence at her side with a look, but though he smiled, he joined Lady St. Cloud on her sofa.

"Daniel, I am so pleased all that bothersome business is finished. Really! As if I wouldn't know my husband's own cousin. You remind me of dear St. Cloud so very much."

Katherine searched Daniel's face hurriedly but saw no

resemblance between this tall, black-haired man and her slender blond father. The comfort the supposed presence of a true relation had momentarily brought her was a surprise. She had not been prepared to take over the estate or bolster her mother's sagging spirits. Her father's calm presence, or a reasonable facsimile thereof, would enable her to return to her role of daughter of the house, prepared to plan menus or inventory the linens, but not to supervise the shearing of the sheep or the planting of the crops.

"Katherine! Katherine, wherever are your manners? Mr. Petersham was speaking to you."

"Sorry, Mama, Mr. Petersham. I'm afraid I was thinking of Papa."

"Understandable, my child," Mr. Petersham said in his ponderous voice. "I only commented that you would be relieved to hand over the running of the estate to your cousin, I'm sure. Nasty business for a gently bred female."

"Yes, of course," Katherine agreed faintly.

"Not that you didn't do a jolly good job of it for a female." Happiness over the outcome of the afternoon's activities was making the normally taciturn Mr. Petersham garrulous. "I'll be here tomorrow with all the papers in order for you to receive the estate into your hands, my lord." He rubbed his hands together gleefully. "Ah, yes. Most satisfactory."

"I shall look forward to it," Daniel said. "I am most fortunate to become owner of such a well-kept estate."

Though his smile was clearly commendation of her management, and she was surprised he would recognize her sentiments at such a moment, Katherine was unhappy. And becoming more than a little worried. Suppose "Cousin" Daniel was a wastrel? She had thought to control the estate and all monies, but it was clear Mr.

Petersham would expect to deal only with her so-called cousin.

"Yes, we are fortunate your shipboard accident did not have more serious consequences," Mr. Petersham added.

Katherine's eyes sharpened. "What accident?" she demanded.

"Nothing to alarm you, Miss St. Cloud. Your cousin was telling us he was knocked overboard only a day out of London. Most disturbing."

Katherine stared at Daniel. "You did not speak of this earlier."

"It seemed of no consequence," Daniel murmured.

Of no consequence! Katherine started to question her so-called cousin at length, but the rising of the three solicitors halted her. She would have to save her inquiry for a later time.

Daniel watched the growing consternation on the young lady's face with amusement. He had wondered how long it would take her to realize the consequences of her action. Added to that was her alarm over his accident. Was she regretting her choice for the role of cousin?

Though the three solicitors left shortly thereafter, Katherine was stymied in her attempts to speak privately with Daniel. Lady St. Cloud urged the young man to have a second cup of tea and talk about himself.

"Last evening, there was such excitement over your arrival, we had no time to speak."

Katherine had made sure of it. She wanted to give the man time to settle into his part before subjecting him to her gentle mother's probing. For all her physical frailty, Lady St. Cloud had never let her daughter forget her duties or escape unscathed from unapproved adventures.

"Tell me about your dear father. I believe he attended our engagement party," she said pensively. "Yes, yes, he did. I'm sure of it. He looked a great deal like my Robert. That's why I was so surprised by your black hair."

"From my mother's side of the family, Lady St. Cloud. She is of French descent. I'm afraid I can tell you little about my father. He died when I was two years of age, and I scarce remember him."

"Oh, you poor child," Lady St. Cloud sympathized, causing Katherine to choke on her tea. "And your poor mother. I know just how she must have felt. My dear Robert was taken from us so suddenly." When she paused, Daniel reached over and squeezed her hand in sympathy. "Dear boy, such a delight," she said to him, smiling tremulously.

Katherine seethed as she watched this stranger charm her mother. She had not intended . . . oh, well, what would it hurt? Her mother, in spite of Katherine's efforts, had seemed unsettled since her father's death. If "dear Daniel" could restore her calm, it was little enough to do for his keep.

"Perhaps your mother will come to live with you. We would welcome her, Daniel," Lady St. Cloud continued.

Daniel ignored his cousin's vigorous head shake. "You are most obliging, madam."

"You must call me Margaret, Daniel. Aunt, if you prefer."

With a warm smile, Daniel lifted her hand to his lips. "Thank you, Aunt Margaret, though you appear much too young to be my aunt."

"Alas, I had hoped to be a grandmama before now, but with Peter taken from us, I must wait for Katherine. And my poor Robert will not be here to enjoy the little ones."

It was in moments like this that Katherine ached for her father. He had been a calm, comforting presence. She moved to her mother's side, clasping her hand. "I think all of this has been too much for you, Mama. Let me assist you to your room."

"Thank you, dear." She turned to the young man beside her. "I will see you at dinner, dear Daniel, and welcome to our family."

"Thank you, Aunt Margaret. You are very generous."

With a sweet smile, the little lady allowed her daughter to help her from her chair. Katherine gave Daniel a hard look as she said, "I'll return in a moment, cousin, and give you a tour of the estate, if you will wait here."

"I'm at your convenience, Cousin Katherine."

Ha! It would be the first time, Katherine thought grimly. He had refused to discuss with her his plans to satisfy the solicitors, in spite of her insistence. Her intent to control this man seemed hopelessly naive now, but the choice had been taken from her.

When she had settled her mother for a repose, Katherine returned to find Daniel standing in the drawing room staring out the window. She studied his tall, muscular form. There was nothing of the dilettante about him. His old-fashioned coat was taut across his broad shoulders and his leather breeches fit snugly to his calves. A shudder of fear over her foolhardiness ran through her.

Something must have alerted him to her presence. He swung around and smiled. "Cousin, you are very prompt. I expected a much longer wait."

With a wave of her hand, Katherine dismissed the pleasantries. "How did you convince them?" she demanded.

"Who? The solicitors?" At her impatient nod, he continued, "I discovered an old bible, as we discussed, and created some family history, that's all."

"But where did you find it? If you got it locally, everyone will know. You should have let Jacob—"

Her protest was halted abruptly as Daniel took hold of her shoulders to give her a brief shake. "Enough, Kate. It is done. Do not worry yourself so."

"But we have conspired to rob the Crown. If we are discovered . . ."

"You must learn to trust me, Katherine. I have been careful. No one will discover our Banbury tale."

His hands warmed her shoulders, but Katherine's nerves were giving way to the strain of the past twenty-four hours. "I must know!" she snapped. "It is up to me to protect my mother! If anything goes wrong . . ." Her lips trembled and her voice rose to a shrill level.

Daniel discovered a more efficacious manner of halting her rising hysteria since his assurances did not soothe her. His lips saluted hers, and the body beneath his hands stilled abruptly. He lifted his head from her soft lips, his glittering blue eyes mere slits as he studied the pale face and lips rounded in surprise.

She awoke from her stupor to tremble with rage. "Unhand me, sir!"

"Are we not kissing cousins, then?" he asked, still retaining his hold.

"No, we are not, as you very well know!" she hissed.

He leaned down again, ignoring her panic, and whispered, "You will bring about the very thing you fear if you are not quiet. You must pretend at all times that I am James Daniel St. Cloud. It is the only way to succeed."

Katherine recognized the wisdom of his words, but his closeness disturbed her. "Release me, please."

"As soon as you promise to abide by my words, bonny Kate."

"I will not speak of this again," she grated. "And do not call me Kate. That is common!"

Stepping back, removing his hands from her shoulders, Daniel smiled. "You could never be considered common, Katherine, even in Canada."

"You are in England now, sir, and you must act like an Englishman," she asserted, feeling more confident now that she had moved beyond his reach.

Something else came to mind. "What of this accident Mr. Petersham mentioned?"

A frown flitted across Daniel's brow. "Nothing to concern you. I was knocked overboard a day's distance from port."

"Knocked? You mean someone deliberately—"

"No! At least, I don't think so. It all happened so quickly. Fortunately, a ship's officer saw me falling and threw a rope to me. I was able to grab hold and he pulled me back aboard."

Katherine stared at him wide-eyed, her mind playing the scene he described. "It is incredible that you were rescued."

"Yes. I would not have been except that we had relatively calm seas. We had not had a single storm the entire sailing."

"You do not often have such accidents, do you?" Katherine questioned anxiously.

"No, sweet cousin," Daniel assured her with a chuckle. "I am no clumsy oaf. You may rest easy on that score."

But the realization that all her careful planning would be for naught should an accident kill Daniel brought tremors of fear to Katherine.

"You are not still worried, are you, my Kate?" Daniel demanded, laughter in his eyes.

"Of course not," she responded with hauteur. "I was thinking of something else." She sought frantically for a new topic, and her eyes lit on his outdated frock coat. "I was considering your appearance. You are a gentleman and must look like one," she said. "I will send a note to my father's tailor. It will not be town-quality, but it will suffice until you go to London."

His black brows rose at her take-charge manner, but he only said, "You may have the dressing of me, if you please, cousin, but no frills or lace. I am too large a man for that."

"We'll see," Katherine said, her eyes tracing his figure until twinkling blue eyes met hers and brought a blush to her cheeks. "We'll take a tour of the stables, shall we?" she suggested hurriedly, very much aware of her new cousin. Though he docilely followed her lead, Katherine felt uneasy about the new addition to her family.

After their tour of the stables, Katherine led the way back to the big house at a fast pace, her lips pursed in displeasure. Even the ripple of leaves in the stately oak trees that lined the path to the house failed to distract her.

"Kate?"

She continued to march, never slowing her pace.

"Katherine?"

When that did not evoke a response, Daniel became even more formal. "Miss St. Cloud?"

"Don't be absurd!" she hissed. Her pace slowed, but she kept her back to her companion. "You are my cousin. You need not address me as Miss St. Cloud when we are alone."

"But when I addressed you as I should, you didn't respond," he reminded her as he grasped her arm.

"Unhand me."

He withdrew the large hand that had halted her progress. "Why are you upset?"

"Because I do not want you to touch me!"

"And before?"

Blue eyes flashed to blue before Katherine turned aside. "I don't know what you mean."

"Yes, you do, my bonny Kate. You stiffened up like a poker. Did I offend you in some way? I swear I did not have that intent."

"Perhaps . . . it is a little unsettling to see someone step into my father's boots so easily." It had also startled Katherine how swiftly the stablehands switched their allegiance to her newfound cousin, accepting him immediately as their master.

Daniel studied the delicate beauty before him. "Or see one's own efforts so easily dismissed?" he offered gently.

Her creamy skin glowed in shame that he should read her thoughts, but she did not answer.

Taking her hand in his large one, Daniel tucked it under his arm and strolled once more toward the house. "You must realize, my Kate, that this part of the estate is a man's world. While I may be able to count linens better than any maid who ever lived, there is not a housewife alive who would take my word for it. The same goes for man's work."

A gurgle of laughter burst from Katherine as she pictured Daniel's muscular figure squeezed into the door of the cupboard with Mrs. Greyson looking on.

"You have forgiven me for being here when your father and brother could not?" he gently prodded.

Lashes sparkling with sudden tears hid her eyes from her escort. "I should be grateful, sir, for your presence. It has saved our home. But . . . I know nothing about you. You could be a—a wastrel . . . or even a murderer!" she exclaimed, that reccurring thought bringing no comfort to an already beleaguered Katherine.

"Did you not consider any of that when you formulated your plan?" Daniel asked, his eyebrows raised in amusement.

"No, I was too intent on saving our home. Mama was becoming more and more distraught and time was growing short. I thought. . . . "

He patted the small hand resting on his arm. "You are too young to carry such a heavy burden. But I am here now, and I promise to protect you and your mother."

The solemnity of his words, as if they were a vow, moved the young woman, who was tired of shouldering a heavy burden alone. It was only later, in her chamber, that she questioned his sincerity.

He charmed everyone. Jacob, Greyson, her mother. Even herself. He must be an accomplished liar. After all, what was he doing here? And how had he kept himself before she had found him? Could a man with no past be trusted? She determined it was her duty to keep watch on this charmer she now called "cousin."

"When were you born, Daniel?" Lady St. Cloud asked at dinner that evening.

"Sixth of August 1788, Aunt Margaret."

"Really? Robert had an August birthday also." She paused to place a minuscule portion of sole in her mouth and chew it thoughtfully before saying, "My, you will be eight and twenty next month. We must have a celebration and introduce you to all the neighbors. Don't you agree, Katherine?"

Katherine, scowling at her plate as if the innocent sole had become a sea monster, started at her mother's words. "Oh, yes, Mama," she agreed automatically.

"We shall begin planning tomorrow."

"I do not want to cause either of you additional

trouble, Aunt Margaret. After all, you have had enough upheaval in your lives in recent months."

Katherine ignored the warm look in Daniel's eyes. But it was difficult to remain on guard in the face of his charm.

"It will be no trouble at all, Daniel. You must meet your new neighbors." An arrested look in her mother's eyes caught Katherine's attention.

"What is it, Mama?"

"What? Oh, nothing, dear." She took a sip of wine before saying brightly, "It is good to have the estate secure again. Have you any sons to follow in your footsteps?"

The rounded innocence of her mother's eyes alerted Katherine, but Daniel was taken aback by the question.

"Sons? Aunt Margaret, I have no wife, much less sons."

"Ah."

Katherine kept her attention focused on her meal. The change of courses from the sole to duckling à l'orange brought a pause.

When the servants departed, Lady St. Cloud commented, "Katherine's birthdate is in October. She should have gone to London for her season last year, as she has already turned nineteen." Katherine felt Daniel's eyes on her, but she remained occupied with her duckling.

Giving a mournful sigh, Lady St. Cloud continued. "Alas, because of our mourning, her presentation must be delayed yet again."

"Never fear, Aunt Margaret. Our Katherine will be just as beautiful a year from now."

Katherine cringed as the other two discussed her as if she were not present. A speculative look in Lady St. Cloud's eyes made her uneasy. Fortunately, her mother changed the subject to Daniel's visit to the stables, and Katherine relaxed.

That evening, as Katherine sat before her mirror while Lucy, her maid, brushed her long blond hair, Lady St. Cloud came to her daughter's room.

"Are you tired, darling?"

"No, Mama, not especially. Was there something you wanted me to do?"

"Why, no, child," the little lady said, patting her daughter on the cheek. "As usual, you have done everything to see to my comfort. I have been blessed with my children."

Katherine frowned in concern. "Should you not go to bed, Mama? I'm afraid all the excitement has been too much for you."

"No, I am fine. I want to talk to you." Her sharp look at Lucy sent the maid scurrying from the room and Katherine's eyebrows soaring.

"Now that we are alone, we may be comfortable," Lady St. Cloud said with a satisfied air. Katherine moved from her vanity to sit beside her mother on the small sofa in front of the fire and waited.

"Daniel is well set up, isn't he? Much taller than your father and Peter. And so considerate. In that, he takes after your father. Robert was quite thoughtful of my feelings."

"I'm glad you are pleased with him, Mama," Katherine said, her deception disturbing her.

"Are not you, Katherine? After all, I believe Daniel will provide for you." Lady St. Cloud smoothed the fringe on her shawl before continuing. "Of course, when Daniel marries, his generosity may be affected."

"I doubt it, Mama. I'm sure Daniel will honor his obligations. You mustn't worry."

"Oh, I don't, child," Mrs. St. Cloud said, patting Katherine's hand. "But I will feel at ease only when your future is settled."

"My future? But Mama, I shall remain here with you, of course," Katherine assured her mother.

"No, Katherine, your future will be with your husband."

"I do not wish to marry, Mama. I will not—"

"Hush, child, of course you will marry. It is the only way to secure your future." She paused again to pull her shawl tighter around her. "And I have decided you should marry Daniel."

Stunned silence followed her pronouncement. Finally, Katherine said, "B-but we are cousins! It is too—"

"Nonsense. You are distant cousins. And a marriage would answer everything. We cannot allow Daniel to dally at his leisure. He must marry at once and produce an heir. If anything happened to him without an heir, we would be lost."

"Yes, but . . . but there are other women."

"Many of them. Every matchmaking mama in the county will be calling here as soon as word is out. But I am not willing to allow control of my home to go to another woman . . . unless it is you, my love."

The most agonizing part of their conversation was that Katherine understood her mother's thinking. If Daniel really were her cousin, such a match would make perfect sense. But to marry this impostor, to whom lies came so easily, was a frightening thought.

"Mama, I cannot—"

"Ssh, child, of course you can. It is your role in life. And it will be so much easier for you. There will be no strange house servants. You will simply become mistress of your own home. Is it not wonderful?"

"W-wonderful, Mama," Katherine said faintly. She

took heart with a second thought. "But perhaps Daniel would prefer to choose his own bride? I'm sure he would, Mama. And, after all, we are in no position to force his hand."

"As if I would ever do such a vulgar thing, Katherine. You should not even speak of such."

"Yes, but Mama—"

"Daniel will listen to me because I am the oldest member of his family, and he will appreciate my guidance."

Not if I talk to him first, Katherine promised herself. "Do not—do not approach him yet, Mama, please. Give me a little longer to—to become accustomed to the idea."

Her mother studied her thoughtfully, and Katherine tried to hide her anxiety. Lady St. Cloud had always been able to detect her falsehoods. "All right, child. A few days I will grant you, but no more. After that, I will make arrangements with Daniel, and you will obey me."

Swallowing the fear that rose up within her, Katherine murmured, "Yes, Mama."

Leaning over to kiss her cheek, Lady St. Cloud said, "Do not look at me that way, child. I am only trying to provide for you in the best way left to me."

A wavering smile was her daughter's only response. As Lady St. Cloud rose and moved toward the door, she said, "I have never told you of my own marriage, have I? I must do so someday." With a faraway look on her face, she bid her daughter good night and wandered away to her room.

Katherine, already dressed in her nightgown and robe, rose stiffly from the sofa and crawled into bed. But though she put her body to rest, she could not stop dealing with her mother's words.

Marry the stranger who had already come to dominate

her life in two short days? Her brother's untimely death and her father's demise had forced Katherine from childhood to adulthood without the attendant romantic illusions. But she was not prepared to marry an unknown stranger.

Of course, this would be strictly a marriage of convenience, contracted to produce an heir immediately. The thought of a child growing in her body was almost as frightening as marriage to a stranger. Katherine shivered beneath the covers. There must be a way to escape such a fate. After all, she had solved the problem of her father's heir. If she put her mind to it, she could come up with an answer to this problem too.

Chapter Three

"Mama," Katherine asked the next morning at the breakfast table, "would you mind if I asked some of my friends to come tomorrow for a picnic? I have not seen anyone in ages, and the weather is wonderfully warm." The bright sun shining through the bow window of the cozy room confirmed Katherine's statement.

Before her mother could voice the protest written on her face, Katherine turned to Daniel. "You would be able to meet some of our neighbors right away. Wouldn't that be wonderful?" As she awaited his response, Katherine examined him for the first time that morning, admiring his well-worn riding clothes. Her mother's proposition of the previous night had caused her to avoid him until now.

"Yes, it would be delightful," Daniel responded.

"Good. I will send the invitations this morning. I'm sure everyone will come. They will all be eager to meet you."

"You won't invite too many, will you, dear?" Lady St. Cloud said, her eyes on the fragile teacup she lowered to its waiting saucer. "I'm not sure Cook is feeling well at the moment."

31

Katherine understood her mother's concern. Only it wasn't for Cook's health. The solution Katherine had discovered for her problem was to provide another young lady with the honor of becoming Lady St. Cloud. Of course, she would have to get a promise from Daniel not to forget his obligations, but there was time for that later. First, she must bait the trap with the most eligible young women in the county.

"Perhaps only a few, like Elizabeth and—and Marcella, and of course there's Sir William and—" Lady St. Cloud continued.

Elizabeth was her closest friend. Though unfashionably plump, she had the merriest chuckle and most understanding smile. Marcella Lewiston, on the other hand, was not well liked and had spots. Katherine knew, in all honesty, that she outshone both in physical beauty, though she counted Elizabeth the most charming. But her mother did not want her to include anyone Daniel might be attracted to, thereby ruining her plan. Best to change the subject.

"Mama, not Sir William, please."

"He is our neighbor, child. We must not be rude."

Katherine sank her teeth into her bottom lip. "But Mama . . . oh, very well."

Her mother's smile of thanks was ruefully acknowledged. Katherine was caught by her own machinations.

Seeing Daniel's curious eye on her, Katherine smoothed out her smile and excused herself from the table. "I'll just go talk to Cook about the menu."

Once Katherine left the table, Daniel concentrated his interest on Lady St. Cloud. "Aunt Margaret, is the entertainment worrisome? I only agreed because I thought it would amuse Katherine."

"It is not that, Daniel." The older woman stared at the

man, frowning before saying, "Could you spare me a few moments?"

"Of course. I am at your service." When she started to rise, Daniel sprang from his chair to assist her.

"Thank you, dear boy. Let's go into my sitting room so we may be more private."

Once seated in a small room drenched in pink silks on a sofa much too fragile for his large frame, Daniel waited patiently for Lady St. Cloud to begin.

"I did not intend to speak so soon, Daniel, but, since you are a man of the world, I am sure you will understand." At his nod, she continued. "When you arrived, my daughter and I were just days from losing our home. I do not want to experience such agony again. And I am too old to be able to provide for my daughter, should such a happening occur."

Daniel smiled at the petite woman before him. "Have no fear, Aunt Margaret. White Oaks will always be your home."

"Thank you, Daniel. But you see, you do not have the power to promise me that."

Frowning, Daniel said, "But I sign the papers today to receive ownership of the estate."

"I know. But you are also bound by the agreement the Crown made with our family. If you die without a male heir, it reverts to the Crown. And my daughter and I will be left without a feather with which to fly."

Daniel sat waiting for the solution she would present.

"The answer to our problem, of course," Lady St. Cloud said calmly, "is for you to marry and produce an heir quickly."

With a rueful grin, Daniel said, "Somehow I thought that might be your solution."

"Do you have a better one?"

"I could take the two of you back to Canada with me.

It is a fine land, Aunt Margaret, and I am able to provide for both of you."

"I'm sure it is, Daniel," she said with a sigh, "but I could not survive the journey. No, I prefer my solution. Do you find it at all appealing?"

With a warm smile, Daniel said, "Never fear, Aunt Margaret. I have every intention of marrying . . . if Katherine will have me."

His simple words brought tears to Lady St. Cloud's eyes and she sighed deeply. "Oh, Daniel, you are such a dear boy. It was so difficult for me to . . ."

He took her small hand in his. "It is all right, Aunt Margaret. You must not worry so."

"Are you sure . . . that is, I do not wish either of you to be unhappy, but I thought. . . ."

"Have you discussed this with Katherine?" Daniel watched her eyes fall away. "She was not pleased?"

"It is not that she . . . that is, she is very young. And she has been both protector and comforter to me. She only asked that I delay speaking to you, and I agreed."

At his raised brows, she hurriedly defended herself. "I intended to keep my promise, but you will meet so many young ladies tomorrow at the picnic, all instructed by their mamas to catch your eye. I feared you might look in another direction."

"Nay, Aunt Margaret, there has been no direction but Katherine's since I first saw her."

Joy broke over the lady's face. "Oh, Daniel, I am so pleased!"

"But," he added with a stern look, "you must allow me to court her in my own way. I'll take no unwilling bride to my bed. Will you give me your word not to discuss our conversation with her?"

"Yes, Daniel, I give you my word. But you will not delay too long?" she couldn't resist asking.

"I will not delay, but . . . I will not have Katherine forced into marriage with me for the price of this estate. There is no need. You must believe that I will provide for the two of you, no matter what her decision."

"Very well, Daniel. But I shall hope and pray that she is wise enough to see what a fine man you are."

With an endearing grin, Daniel said, "I can't wait for you to meet my mother. She will greatly admire your taste."

The replies to the picnic invitations were swift and unanimous. The entire neighborhood was agog to see the man who had saved the St. Clouds from ruin.

One particular invitation was answered in person. Elizabeth Drake was Katherine's best friend, but though their estates marched side by side, it had been several weeks since they had met.

"Betsy!" Katherine squealed when Greyson escorted the young lady into the back sitting room where Katherine was planning the details of her picnic.

After a hug, Elizabeth gave her best curtsy, swinging wide her sunny sprigged muslin skirts, and said, "I've come to inform you, Miss St. Cloud, that I accept your invitation for dining alfresco tomorrow." Her pursed lips twitched as her friend burst into laughter.

"Betsy, you are such a card. You sounded exactly like Sir William at his most pompous." Katherine's beaming face belied the solemnity of her gray gown, representing her half-mourning.

"Thank you, thank you, thank you," Betsy said with another grandiose curtsy.

"Come, sit down and tell me your news. I have not seen you for an age."

Elizabeth joined her friend on the sofa. "Your news sounds more exciting. I was thrilled to hear your cousin arrived in time to rescue you."

Katherine shifted her eyes. "Yes, it is marvelous, isn't it?"

"What are you hiding?"

Her eyes flying back to her friend's face, Katherine thought frantically. "It is only that . . . Mama wants me to marry him."

Elizabeth's lips formed a perfect "O" but no sound came out. Finally, she whispered, "Is he that horrid?"

"No, of course not!" Katherine snapped. "It's nothing like that. He is quite . . . quite charming. And handsome," she added.

"But you don't want to marry him?" Elizabeth asked, feeling her way.

Katherine jumped from the sofa to stride about the room, a habit her mother deplored. "I don't want to marry at all."

"You don't?" Elizabeth asked, surprised. "But Katherine . . ."

"Do you?"

"Why, of course I do, Katherine! I can't wait to be mistress of my own establishment, have babies. . . ." A dreamy look filled her eyes.

"Well, I can wait," Katherine said stubbornly.

"What are you going to do? Will your mother insist?"

"I have a plan. That is the reason for the picnic. I shall find a bride for my cousin. Would you like to marry him? I would love to have you live here."

Elizabeth's cheeks suffused with pink. "He would never look at me. Besides . . . I am . . . interested in another."

"What?" Katherine shrieked. "And you have not told me? Who is it? Are you affianced?"

"No! No one knows. He does not return my regard, Katherine. We are only friends, but I dream. This spring, with all the fashionable ladies in London, I danced with him several times at the county gatherings."

"While I was in black gloves and did not attend! And you have yet to tell me his name."

With another blush, Elizabeth said, "You know him well. It is Jack." Jack Burford was the squire's only son, a burly young man with gentle manners, a great favorite among the young people.

"But I thought he . . ." Katherine caught herself before finishing her thought, but Elizabeth knew what she had been about to say.

"I know. He yearns for Lady Priscilla. But she has been in London all season. I'm hoping he may see her as she is when she returns."

"She is back now. I received her acceptance only minutes before your arrival."

"Oh."

At her friend's downcast face, Katherine reached out to squeeze her hand. "Don't despair. Jack cannot possibly prefer her shallowness to your sweet face."

"You mean my pudding face to her beauty."

"I mean no such thing. You are delightfully round, not all angles and bones. Besides, Lady Priscilla will have no time for Jack when she sees Daniel."

"Why ever not? Jack is most handsome." Elizabeth ruffled up like a hen protecting her chick.

"Do you want her to prefer Jack, you silly goose?" Katherine asked with a grin.

"Of course not," Elizabeth responded, horrified.

"Then we will push her in Daniel's direction." A new thought struck Katherine. "Oh, no. That means I would have to live with her. Oh, dear."

"How terrible. Perhaps he will be attracted to someone else. Who have you invited?"

The two young ladies bowed their heads over the invitation list to determine Daniel's future bride.

Daniel kept his eyes on Katherine as she moved among her neighbors, the light breeze fluttering the lilac muslin trimmed in black that she wore. Her straw bonnet, hyacinths on its brim, shielded her face from the late morning sun . . . and from him.

He had earlier been introduced to all the young people of the district by Katherine with great enthusiasm. In fact, Katherine had encouraged him to sit with the young lady beside him, who had droned on about her successful season in London for almost an hour now.

"La, Lord St. Cloud, you would not believe the entertainment in London. Every evening, there are several balls and musicales to choose from. Some evenings I have attended as many as four balls. Of course, my family is of the first stare and in demand everywhere," Lady Priscilla Davenport assured Daniel, fluttering her lashes down in mock modesty, hoping it would draw attention to her flawless complexion and the pale green walking dress brought straight from London. When there was no response, her eyes came back to her audience to find him watching his cousin. "My lord?"

"I beg your pardon, Lady Priscilla. I am concerned that my cousin might need my assistance."

"Oh, you mustn't concern yourself with Katherine. She's a capable female." Her titter of laughter did not please Daniel.

Turning frosty blue eyes on his companion, he said, "Excuse me, Lady Priscilla. I am quite sure my cousin needs my assistance."

"But I don't think. . . ." Lady Priscilla trailed off as

she was abandoned by the gentleman of her choice. She swiftly searched for a replacement, her eyes lighting upon young Burford a short distance away. His conversation with Elizabeth was no hindrance to her need. "Oh, Jack?"

The young man's head whipped around and, with a hurried apology to Elizabeth, he eagerly leapt to his feet and came to Lady Priscilla's side. Though he was not as impressive as the guest of honor, in a brown hunting jacket and fawn breeches Mr. Burford made a creditable escort. Elizabeth sighed deeply as she watched him depart before striking up a conversation with her nearest neighbor.

Katherine turned from speaking with one of the servants to see Daniel approaching her while Lady Priscilla had Jack at her side. "Now look what you've done!" she protested to Daniel.

"What have I done, my Kate?"

"You have broken Betsy's heart!"

"I have?" he said in surprise. "I thought her interest lay in other quarters."

"Of course it does," she grumbled, "though I'm sure I don't know how you are aware of it. But you have allowed him to be entrapped by Lady Priscilla."

Daniel grinned in comprehension. "Ah. Shall I go rescue the lad?"

"Oh, never mind," Katherine grumbled as she directed the servants to spread the cloths and lay out Cook's offerings. They were only a short distance from the big house in a wide, grassy meadow beside a bubbling stream. Several shade trees provided relief from an unusually bright sun. It was one of Katherine's favorite spots.

"May I be of assistance, Miss St. Cloud?"

Katherine turned to find Sir William, his chest puffed

out in importance, standing next to Daniel. With restraint, she said, "Thank you, sir, but my cousin has already offered. Really, there's nothing to be done." Katherine fought against the comparison of the two men beside her. Daniel was commanding, at ease in a charcoal gray jacket over black breeches. Sir William was at a disadvantage with his overstuffed figure in pale breeches that appeared near to bursting and a bright yellow waistcoat that did not enhance his florid complexion, topped by an ill-fitting brown jacket.

"Should you have a need, I am at your service," the man persisted.

"Thank you, Sir William," she repeated, avoiding his eyes.

"Are you adapting to our ways?" Sir William asked, turning to Daniel with a sneer.

"I'm fairly adaptable," Daniel assured the man, refusing to take offense.

Sir William grunted in response before saying, "I do not see any resemblance between you and this Canadian, Miss St. Cloud."

Katherine's small gasp was not noticed by the two men, who stared at each other, Daniel in amusement and Sir William in irritation.

"Really?" Daniel responded in Katherine's stead.

His brief answer left Sir William with nothing to say. With a curt nod, he stomped off.

"Be careful," Katherine warned with a whisper. "He is not a fool."

"Do not worry, my Kate. I will protect you," Daniel assured her, his smile warm upon her face.

Katherine stared up at him until one of the servants approached, requiring her attention. "Oh, yes, please, Lewis, you may begin serving. My cousin will call everyone to dinner."

Daniel did as she wished, remnants of his smile still on his face. Lady Priscilla, who had determined to snub him the next time he approached her, found herself smiling at him in return.

The next morning Katherine sat over her second cup of tea awaiting Daniel's arrival at the breakfast table. He did not appear to be the type to sleep the day away, as she had heard the dandies did in London. But he had not yet come down, and she was becoming impatient. He had told her mother last night he had enjoyed the picnic, meeting his neighbors, but that was not enough.

Lady St. Cloud had made it impossible for Katherine to speak privately with Daniel the night before, demanding she retire along with her mother. But Lady St. Cloud was never an early riser, and Katherine hoped to corner Daniel at the breakfast table. She had to determine if Daniel had an interest in Lady Priscilla, who had appeared to dominate his time at the picnic. Not that she had really paid it that much attention, she assured herself.

"Miss Katherine," Greyson said, interrupting her thoughts. "Sir William has called to see you. I left him in the Green Salon."

"Thank you, Greyson," Katherine said while she tried to think why the man would be calling so early. Rising from the table and smoothing down her gray skirts, she said, "Should my cousin come down, please ask him to join us." She wanted no tête-à-tête with Sir William.

"Good morning, Sir William," Katherine said, seating herself on the brocade sofa with its ridiculous crocodile feet. Her mother had bought it during the Egyptian craze that had dominated French fashion after Napoleon's foray there.

The man reseated himself in a nearby gilt chair before

saying, "I have come this morning on serious business. When I asked to see your mother, Greyson said she had not yet arisen."

"My mother is in fragile health. In general, I deal with any difficulties."

"Very well, since it concerns you, I suppose that will be sufficient."

Katherine's raised eyebrows were her response.

"Two years ago, I offered for you and asked for the land that marches alongside mine for your dowry. I knew you were young, but I wanted your father to know of my interest. I do not know if he informed you."

"He did." Her frozen response did not appear to affect her guest.

"Good. I have come to repeat my offer." There was a self-satisfied air about him that incited in Katherine a desire to slap his face. However, her years of training under her mother's eagle eye stood her in good stead.

"I am honored by your offer, Sir William, but regretfully, I must decline."

"You had best take my offer, girl. Should this so-called cousin decamp with your valuables, you'll find yourself left at the marketplace."

"How dare you speak to me in such a fashion, sir! I will ring for Greyson to show you the door and . . ." She stood and moved to the bellpull.

"I think he's a fake," Sir William said, rising, his bottom lip stubbornly jutting out over his protruding stomach.

His words stopped Katherine in her tracks. What did he know? "Why would you say such a thing?"

"Well, for one thing, he's dark, not blond like you St. Clouds."

"His mother is a Frenchwoman from Quebec. He

lived in Montreal, and that is why it took so long to find him."

"I suppose that is why the entries in the bible were in French," Sir William muttered.

"Were they?" Katherine involuntarily asked, then caught herself. "Yes, of course that is why."

"Well, even if he is your cousin, he could be a scoundrel. Those are the types who run off to the New World."

"Oh? I thought those were the brave adventurers, ready to face the unknown," Katherine challenged, a determined light in her eyes.

Sir William stared at the young woman facing him, her cheeks flushed and her blue eyes fierce. He wanted her. And had done so for several years. But he also wanted a fair price if he was going to marry the chit. "I believe I shall talk to your cousin. After all, this brave adventurer, as you call him, is head of the family now. I'm sure, since you admire him so," he said with a sneer, "you are willing to leave the decision in his hands."

"I hope my cousin has faith in my caring for her," a quiet voice said from the doorway, causing both occupants of the salon to jump. The sight of Lord St. Cloud dressed in riding clothes leaning against the doorjamb brought relief to Katherine, but not to her guest. "Good day, Sir William. What decision am I to make for my cousin?"

"I have come here with an honorable offer of marriage."

Daniel's eyes flickered over his cousin, resting momentarily on her anxious eyes. "I'm sure my cousin is honored by your admiration for her, Sir William, but—"

"You have not heard my offer. I am willing to forgo any money for her dowry. I ask only the five hundred acres of land that march alongside my estate. The land means less to you than the blunt, I'm sure. Not a bad deal, as you can see. I'll even allow the old lady to live with us. Then you will be rid of both your tiresome responsibilities at once." What Daniel assumed was a smile was plastered on Sir William's flaccid face.

"My tiresome responsibilities, as you so graciously called them, I find delightful. And I would never sell my cousin to save a few pounds. She is much too precious for that."

"Ah, fancy her yourself, do you?" Sir William said with a curl of his lip.

"Katherine," Daniel murmured, ignoring their guest, "go ask Greyson to come here."

Though she knew Daniel wanted to be rid of her, Katherine considered using the bellpull to summon Greyson. She felt she had the right to hear when it was her fate at hand. But the pale rigidity of Daniel's face had her obeying his words. Lingering in the hall, she saw Sir William routed immediately upon Greyson's entry to the salon. His pale face, lips pressed tightly together, made her wonder what Daniel had said to the man.

As soon as Greyson and Sir William had gone down the hall, Katherine slipped back into the Green Salon. She discovered Daniel still leaning against the wall just inside the door. "Are you angry?" she demanded, her eyes registering his whitened features.

"With you? No, of course not."

"I meant with Sir William," she explained before adding, "And thank you for refusing his offer so emphatically."

"I'm glad you are pleased. Perhaps you would inform your mother of what has transpired. I don't think she will disagree with us, but she should be informed."

"Yes, of course, I will." Katherine waited, studying

him. Something was not quite right, but she couldn't put her finger on it.

"Perhaps you would do so now?" Daniel said pleasantly, but there was an insistence in his tone that puzzled her.

"Have you had breakfast? I shall tell Greyson to brew a fresh pot of—"

"Katherine, go!" Daniel almost shouted just as Greyson came back into the room accompanied by a stout footman.

"Here, sir," the old butler said, rushing to the young man's side. "You must be seated at once."

Katherine stared as Daniel's tall, lean body sagged against the wall, to be swiftly shored up by Greyson. The footman hurried to take the bulk of the weight on his young shoulders and the two men guided Daniel to the sofa.

"But . . . what is the matter?" Katherine demanded.

A heaving Greyson said, "The Master had an accident while riding this morning."

Having seen him ride the day before, Katherine knew him to be well at home on a horse. "What happened?"

"It appears his saddle gave way as he took a fence."

"Good Lord, you could have been killed, Daniel! You should be in bed."

"And that is where I am going if you will kindly remove yourself as I asked," Daniel muttered.

"Well, I will, but I don't see why you didn't go straight to bed instead of coming in here," Katherine grumbled, staring at Daniel in frustration.

"I thought you needed me."

Daniel's simple response stayed in Katherine's mind as she saw him comfortably settled and sent for the doctor in spite of his protests.

Dr. Benjamin assured her he would recover after a day and night spent in bed. Katherine then did what she had wanted to do from the first. She hurried for the stables. "Jesse?" she called as she entered the gloomy interior, seeking the man who had overseen her father's stables all her life.

"Right 'ere, Miss Katherine," a seemingly detached voice called before an old man with a strong back stepped from the tack room. "I been expectin' you."

"What happened?"

"Young Jem, the lad I hired just last year, saddled the Master's horse this mornin'. He used a saddle he was supposed to 'ave mended. But I checked, miss. He never mended it."

"Where is he?" Katherine demanded tersely.

"Gone."

"You fired him?"

"Never 'ad the chance, miss. When the Master's horse came back riderless was the last time I seen him. When I found the Master and checked the leather, I looked for 'im right away, but he'd already gone."

"Where would he have gone?"

"He always talked of America, but he don't 'ave any blunt. I reckon he just run off so's he wouldn't be punished."

"All right, Jesse."

"Tell the Master it won't happen again, I promise. An' tell him I'm sorry."

"I will." Katherine walked slowly back to the house, thinking as she went. What happened was an accident, of course. Jem wouldn't be the first servant to run away, afraid of his master's retribution for a job poorly done.

But it was a frightening thought that all her worries and planning could be for nothing if an accident killed the impostor now. The fact that this was his second brush

with death in less than two weeks added to her fears.
Was such a coincidence possible? Or was someone
interested in Daniel's early demise?

That thought sent shivers down Katherine's spine. She
could see no connection between the two events. But she
must be on her guard. If only she knew what she should
guard against!

Katherine was also surprised to discover she was
becoming quite attached to Daniel. Almost as if he really
were her cousin. His simple response to her question
came back to her. She would return the favor, she
staunchly decided, squaring her shoulders. She would do
her best to ensure no more accidents occurred . . . if
she could.

Chapter Four

Returning to the house in a pensive mood, Katherine was roused by the sight of Greyson. "One moment, Greyson. Had Lord St. Cloud been discovered before Sir William's arrival?"

"Oh, yes, Miss Katherine. He was up and about at the crack of dawn. He was brought to the house before you finished your breakfast."

Staring at the old retainer, Katherine asked, "Why was I not informed?" The chill in her tone wiped the smile from Greyson's face.

"The Master said not to bother you, miss."

Katherine sank her teeth into her bottom lip, a taste of bitterness in her mouth. It galled her that a stranger she had introduced into the household could supersede her authority in only four days. "I see. And you informed Lord St. Cloud that Sir William had called?"

"You asked that he join you, Miss Katherine," Greyson said reproachfully.

"Not from his sickbed!" Katherine exclaimed.

"Now, Miss Katherine, don't become overset," the old man said, just as he had when Katherine was a child.

48

Heaving a sigh, Katherine said, "All right, thank you, Greyson."

When she was alone in the hallway, Katherine thought for a moment before turning to hurry up the stairs. She moved purposefully down the hallway and rapped on a door. When the door opened partway and Jacob's head appeared, she asked, "How is Lord St. Cloud?"

"Very well, Miss Katherine. He is resting now."

"Is he asleep?" she persisted.

"No, Miss Katherine, just resting."

"Good. I want to speak to him." She pushed against the door but met with resistance.

"Miss Katherine, you cannot enter a gentleman's chamber! Your mother would never allow it."

"Jacob, open this door. I am mistress here!"

"The Master said—"

"Do not call him that! You of all people—"

"Katherine!" The deep voice stopped both combatants in their tracks, with Katherine very much aware of her indiscretion.

The next time that voice of authority spoke, it was much calmer. "Let her in, Jacob."

The valet's face disappeared from Katherine's view as she heard him say, "But, sir . . ."

She didn't hear any response from Daniel, but the door swung open to her and she stepped into what had been her father's rooms. The curtains were drawn and there was only a single candle to dispel the gloom, but Katherine had no difficulty seeing the man Jacob was propping up in the big bed with several pillows. She stared in fascination.

Katherine had never seen a man other than her Papa or Peter in less than proper attire. Daniel's big body seemed to go on forever. Her eyes were drawn to the open shirt and the black curly hair on his broad chest.

"That will be all, Jacob." Katherine jumped in surprise at his voice.

"But, sir, Miss . . . " Jacob protested.

Again, no additional words were spoken, but Jacob acquiesced. Katherine did not blame him after seeing Daniel's cold stare. When the door closed behind the man, Daniel gestured to a chair near the bed, but Katherine ignored him and moved to his bedside.

The candle lit up her golden hair and the pure white of her morning gown, making the man wonder if he had died and was in the presence of an angel.

"What is it, Katherine?" he asked, to erase such a romantic notion.

"I wanted to see if you were all right."

"Jacob could've told you that."

"Yes, but I wanted to be sure," Katherine said lamely, unable to explain the need to see with her own eyes her supposed cousin's recovery. She backed away from his magnetic presence and sat down in the chair.

Daniel frowned. "Thank you for your concern, but I shall be up and about in no time. You must return to your normal duties and forget all about my insignificant accident."

"You cannot be serious. Do you not realize how frightening this was for me—us, as well as you? I constructed this entire plot to save our home for my mother. And now, because of a careless accident, we might yet lose everything! It would kill my mother. And you say I must forget it?"

"Katherine, I have no intention of meeting an early death. You must not become overset."

"Why?"

"Because you tend to become hysterical . . . and indiscreet." There was a smile playing about his firm lips that fascinated her.

"I know," she admitted, her eyes falling, "but with good reason, surely? This is your second accident in less than a month. Does that not concern you?"

"Accidents happen, Katherine. There can be no significance between the two."

"But . . ."

"My dear, I know you are concerned about your future, but I promise I will provide for you and your mother. And at this point, you have no choice but to trust me, do you?"

"Until you marry and provide us a male heir." Daniel's eyes never left her face and Katherine felt her cheeks grow warm. "Did you . . . are you interested in any of the young women you met yesterday?"

"Yes."

Katherine swallowed. She hadn't expected that response. With inexplicable trepidation, she asked, "Anyone in particular?"

"Yes."

She waited, but he said nothing else, just watched her with a smile on his lips.

"In whom are you interested?" she demanded stiffly.

"That is something which need not concern you, my dear Katherine. At least not yet."

"You will let us know before you place a stranger above us in our own home, won't you, dear cousin?" Katherine said bitterly, miffed at being shut out by this man who owed his present position to her.

"I am feeling very tired," Daniel said with a sigh, reminding Katherine of his accident even as he ignored her last remark. "Before you go, however, I wish you to come closer."

With a mixture of worry and frustration, Katherine left her chair. She had no choice but to comply with his request. When she stood beside him, he motioned with a finger for her to bend to him. Assuming he wished to whisper some secret to her, Katherine bent down, unconscious of the expanse of bosom presented to the patient's view.

His indrawn breath caused her to whisper, "Are you in pain?"

"Yes, sweet Katherine, I am." Without further words, a strong hand took her chin and pulled her face closer, and firm lips covered hers in a gentle kiss.

When Katherine opened her eyes wide to stare at him after his kiss, he smiled and said, "Now, my bonny Kate, you know a little of the danger of entering a man's bedchamber. Be off with you before your mother finds out."

Katherine snapped out of the trance that had held her and scurried from the room, her cheeks bright banners of her embarrassment. Her supposed cousin was much too full of himself, she thought firmly, ignoring the sensation his lips had aroused in her.

Katherine found her thoughts a jumble of confusion the rest of the day. Anger with Daniel, worry about their precarious position, curiosity about which young lady he had meant—all led immediately back to the kiss he had taken. However, when Daniel appeared for dinner, worry was the predominant emotion.

"Why are you out of your bed?" she whispered sharply just before her mother entered the Blue Salon where they awaited their summons to dinner.

There was no opportunity for Daniel to explain his presence, but the glimmer of laughter in his eyes told Katherine he would not have tried. As Greyson announced their meal before Lady St. Cloud could be seated, Daniel offered each of the ladies an arm and led them to the dining room.

Lady St. Cloud sighed as Greyson seated her at the

walnut table that seated twelve. "Isn't it amazing how more like a family we seem with Daniel's presence?"

"Yes, Mama," Katherine murmured, avoiding Daniel's smile.

They were halfway through their meal when Katherine realized her mother had scarcely eaten anything. "Mama, are you feeling quite the thing?"

"I am fine, my dear. I just have no appetite this evening."

"Is anything worrying you?" Katherine asked, though her mother's serene countenance showed no signs.

"No, not at all. In fact, since Daniel's arrival, I feel quite confident of your future."

"Thank you, Aunt Margaret, for your confidence in me," Daniel inserted.

There seemed to be some significance in her mother's words, but Katherine refused to consider it. "I am glad, Mama. You have had too much worry the past few years."

With a faint smile, Lady St. Cloud said, "No more than you, child, and you have been so strong for both of us. I am glad Daniel may now shoulder the burden."

Her mother's words made Katherine grateful she had devised her scheme. But the morning's happenings underlined the fragility of her plan. And if her mother had any idea that Daniel was not in reality her cousin, her serenity would be shattered.

After escorting her mother to her bedchamber, Katherine slipped back down to the sitting room where they had left Daniel. "The doctor said you were supposed to remain abed," she said as she entered the room.

"Why, Katherine, I thought you had retired for the evening," Daniel said mockingly, causing Katherine to grind her teeth.

"Well, I have not! But you should have. Why have you not gone upstairs?"

"Because, sweet cousin, I felt sure you would rest better if you had the opportunity to enumerate my sins. Shall we take a stroll in the garden? There is a full moon and more privacy among the roses."

His casual air only irritated Katherine more, but the significance of his remark about privacy was not lost on her. Taking his arm, she kept her silence until they had strolled a distance from the house. The heady perfume of the roses encircled them, and the liquid silver of the moonlight gave the blooms and her companion a fairy sheen. Though she continued to chastise him, her voice softened.

"Tease me if you will, Daniel, but the doctor said—"

"I know precisely what the doctor said, my Kate. I may have received a knock on the head, but my brain was not addled." His warm smile reassured Katherine.

"You are sure—"

"I am in excellent health," he interrupted, "but your concern heartens me greatly."

Katherine noted a certain gleam in the man's eyes that she had seen earlier when he kissed her. She retreated a step and was surprised at her disappointment when he did not follow. "It is only because we would lose the estate if something happened to you," she said abruptly.

"Then it is fortunate that I have an exceedingly hard head, is it not?" Daniel asked with a wry smile.

Her rudeness embarrassed Katherine and she sought another topic of conversation. "Since you are recovered from your accident, perhaps you will consent to a fitting session with my father's tailor."

"Gladly. I traveled lightly on the trip over. And I will even concede that our idea of fashion is not on the same level as your expertise." His admiring eyes traveled over

Katherine's gown, another of her gray silks, this one cut low across her shoulders and clinging to her well-rounded figure.

Katherine jumped as he stretched out an arm toward her, but he was only reaching for a pink blossom. With a snap, he broke the rose from its stem and placed it in the deep vee of her gown.

"I—I will arrange it," Katherine gasped. Then, with a muffled good night, she turned and raced up the path to the safety of the brightly lighted house and her bedchamber.

Why was she acting like a frightened child? she demanded of herself. The man had only to look at her to send her fleeing from his presence.

Several minutes of pacing brought no answers, and Katherine plopped down in disgust at her desk to write a note to the tailor. She then made a list of what she thought Daniel's wardrobe should include. When she caught herself dwelling on the image of his muscular form, she put away her lists and sought her bed. But the lingering warmth of his fingers against her skin told her she would be wise to avoid the combination of moonlight and the dangerous man she called "cousin."

Lucy found her mistress quite fussy over her appearance the next morning, an unusual occurrence. Her hair must be arranged just so, and she changed her gown three times. Lucy understood the difficulty, even if Katherine did not.

Their care was rewarded with Daniel's admiring glance when Katherine entered the breakfast room.

"Oh! You're feeling better? I did not expect you to be up so early," Katherine said, her cheeks rosy.

"I'm glad I am. Your appearance can only improve my health."

"Thank you, kind sir," Katherine said with a pleased smile. "You are sure you're feeling well enough to be fitted for a new wardrobe this morning?"

"Of course, though I must speak with Mr. Cullum."

"Mr. Cullum?" Katherine asked in surprise. "Is anything wrong?" Cullum was the manager of their estate, and Katherine had worked closely with him for the past six months.

"No, nothing is wrong. I just want to understand the operation of the farm. And there are some new farming techniques I would like to discuss with him."

Katherine bristled at the idea of any change. "We are quite prosperous the way things are. My father was an excellent manager."

"I am not criticizing your father, Katherine," Daniel said gently. "But that does not mean that we must continue to do everything the way it has always been done."

"I don't see why not," Katherine said stubbornly.

Daniel's amused smile did nothing to smooth her ruffled feathers. "Perhaps because I am now in charge and I want to try something new."

Katherine jumped from her chair and moved to where Daniel was seated at the table. "You are not in charge!" she hissed. "You work for me, and you'd best not forget it!"

Without rising, Daniel pulled Katherine down to him and thoroughly kissed her. Katherine's disoriented look and shaky limbs made it difficult to stand after he released her.

"Y-you mustn't do that," she insisted, backing away. She found his touch disturbing . . . and mesmerizing.

"But that is your punishment each time you forget," Daniel said with a grin.

"That—that is outrageous! You have no right

to . . ." Katherine broke off as Greyson entered the room with a fresh pot of tea.

"Good morning, Miss Katherine, my lord."

"Good morning, Greyson," she said in strangled tones.

"Good morning, Greyson," Daniel said.

"Are you feeling quite the thing, Miss Katherine?" the old butler asked in concern.

"Yes, yes, I'm fine," Katherine said hurriedly. She could hardly explain that her plan was backfiring on her. She retook her seat and concentrated on the meal Greyson was dishing up for her.

"Should you require anything else, my lord, please ring," Greyson told Daniel.

After the old man's departure, Daniel began eating as if nothing were wrong. "How can you sit there calmly eating as if you had not betrayed me!" Katherine demanded.

"How have I betrayed you?"

"You are pretending to be the owner of White Oaks."

There was a serious look on Daniel's face as he leaned toward the fuming young woman. "No, Katherine, I *am* the owner of White Oaks."

"Only because I lied for you!" she spat at him.

"However it came about, cousin, I am the owner and I have the papers to prove it. I have no intention of betraying you, but you must not question my authority."

His tone caused Katherine to tremble. She stared at Daniel as she realized how thoroughly she had betrayed herself. Through her desperate charade, she had passed legal control of her home into a stranger's hands, and there was nothing she could do about it now.

Daniel ignored her dismay and sank his even white teeth into one of the orange muffins for which Cook was

famous. "Mmm, this is delicious. It's amazing you're so
small with such a good cook."

When there was no response, Daniel cocked his head
and smiled. "Come on, Kate, I promise to care for you.
Is it really so tragic if I change from wheat to oats in the
east field?"

"It is not that and you know it."

"Then what is it? The realization that you have created
a monster with your little plan? That you have no control
over me?"

"Yes," Katherine whispered.

Daniel stretched out his hand across the table. "Little
cousin, I am a man of honor. I will care for you as surely
as your father or brother would have done. But I can only
give you my word. It is you who must decide to believe
me."

Though the look on her face remained troubled,
Katherine could not resist the sincerity of his plea, and
her hand stole across the table to meet his halfway. His
weathered fingers curled around hers in a most comforting manner, and he rewarded her effort with a warm
smile. She wanted with all her heart to believe him.
After all, the alternatives were unthinkable.

"Thank you, my bonny Kate. Now, take your breakfast, or you will not have the energy to deck me out as a
man of fashion."

Without another word, Katherine pecked at her food,
though her eyes frequently surveyed her companion
under the veil of her lashes.

Greyson reentered the breakfast room. "Sir, this letter
arrived a few moments ago. Shall I put it in your study,
or would you care to see it now?"

Greyson's behavior only underlined Katherine's earlier discovery. She no longer had control over anything

in the household. Daniel held out his hand for the envelope and Greyson departed.

"This is addressed to all of us, so I assume it is an invitation. Would you care to peruse it?" Daniel asked.

"I'm sure the master of the house should do that," Katherine said, unable to keep her bitterness out of her voice.

Daniel sighed but made no comment, ripping open the envelope. "Ah, it seems we are invited to a small dinner party tomorrow evening."

Katherine waited, but he did not go on. When she looked up, he was watching her with a twinkle in his blue eyes. "Is it appropriate for the master to accept without consulting the other members of his family?"

"Of course not!" she snapped.

"Then perhaps you should look at it."

Katherine snatched the paper from his hands. She knew she was not behaving in a ladylike manner, but this man would try anyone's patience. She read the invitation, her teeth nibbling on her bottom lip. The author of the note was Lady Crane, Lady Priscilla's mother. Katherine flashed a look at Daniel, who was watching her with round-eyed innocence, a look she knew better than to trust.

"Isn't that kind of Lady Crane, when I have not yet met her?"

"We intended to introduce you to the neighbors," Katherine said, a trifle defensively.

"Well, now, Lady Crane will save you the effort by doing so tomorrow evening. Will most everyone be there?"

"I do not know. She says a small entertainment, but there are not that many families in the neighborhood. We are a sparsely settled lot." Katherine paused to consider her neighbors. "I do hope Betsy will be there."

"And the ever popular Jack Burford?"

"Oh, the squire and his family will be there. Squire Burford is quite well-to-do. And well liked by everyone," Katherine quickly added, in case Daniel thought she only judged a person by his wealth.

"And Sir William?"

Katherine had forgotten she might be required to face that distasteful gentleman again. Her face reflected her feelings.

"Do not be concerned, Kate. Sir William will not approach you again."

"How can you be sure?"

There was a knowing grin on Daniel's face. "Because I promised him a facer the next time he did so."

"You threatened him?" Katherine demanded, knowing she should be horrified at such behavior but was secretly pleased.

Daniel shrugged his shoulders. "I wanted to be sure he understood my position."

Katherine stared at Daniel in awe. There were some benefits to her plan, she decided.

"Will there be others there whom I have not met?"

"Oh, yes, there will be Mrs. Brody. You will like her, I think. Her husband was in trade and she is fabulously wealthy, but she . . . that is, her speech reflects her birth," Katherine said with a grin. "Lord Crane has great respect for her wealth and forces Lady Crane to tolerate her at all their entertainments. But truly, she is a very likeable person."

"She sounds most delightful," Daniel agreed with a grin.

"And the Reverend and Mrs. Milhouse are always in attendance. He is a little prosy but she is sweet. And, of course, the parents of all the young people you met at the picnic."

"It sounds quite a large gathering."

"Well, it is, but I suppose it does not seem like it to Priscilla and the Cranes. After all, they have just returned from London. To hear Lady Priscilla talk, you would think the entire world could be found in London."

"Do you desire a London season?" The concern in Daniel's voice caused Katherine to eye him in surprise.

"No," she said thoughtfully, "I don't think so. I would like to go to London someday, but a season simply means you are being offered to the highest bidder."

"Somehow I don't think your mother would approve of such a remark."

"Of course she wouldn't," Katherine agreed, "but then, she did not hear it . . . unless you mean to be a tattletale."

Daniel grinned in response to Katherine's smile. It had been sadly lacking this morning. "I promise I will not."

As Katherine buttered a slice of bread, another thought occurred to her. "I suppose you'll have the opportunity to see the young lady in whom you are interested also."

Daniel noted her sharp look and concentrated on his kidneys and eggs. "I suppose so," he agreed indifferently.

"Lady Crane might even have dancing. Do you dance, cousin?"

"I have been known to do so. Montreal has a modicum of entertainment."

"But many of the dances will be country dances, and I am afraid you will not know the movements. Would you like me to teach you?"

There was a flicker of light in Daniel's eyes as he said in disinterested tones, "I suppose you might do so. After all, I would not want to miss the opportunity to dance with the young lady who has drawn my attention."

"I do not see why you will not reveal her name to me!" Katherine protested.

"Love is a delicate flower that must be protected until it reaches full bloom."

"That almost sounds like poetry," Katherine said in surprise. "Are you a poet?"

Daniel grinned. "Possibly. Love can make the most hardened cynic a poet, my dear girl."

"Hmmm, I think you may be misleading me. Am I being teased, cousin?"

Daniel reached over and squeezed her hand. "Perhaps just a little, my Kate."

And also distracted from her original question, the identity of the young woman, she realized. "Shall I arrange to teach you the dances this afternoon? I could ask Betsy Drake to provide the music for us, if that is all right."

"If Miss Drake is willing to assist us, I will put myself at your disposal. You might also invite Mr. Burford to show me the finer nuances of the man's role, you know. That might make Miss Drake's labor the more enjoyable."

"That is a masterful idea, Daniel!" Katherine enthused. She had been thinking about ways to help Betsy engage Jack's attention. "I will write notes to both of them at once." Katherine fairly danced from the room, a smile on her dimpled cheeks.

Daniel rose as she left, and then sank back down into his chair. His love was more interested in her friend's romance than her own admirers, he thought ruefully. But at least that meant she did not encourage offers. Otherwise, he would be at odds with half the county. Because, from his point of view, Katherine St. Cloud was irresistible.

Chapter Five

It was difficult for Daniel to manage a serious conference with Mr. Cullum that day. Katherine had him standing in front of his looking glass for an hour while she and the tailor discussed the garments necessary to an English gentleman. She also insisted the man deliver the new outfit for the Cranes' party the next evening.

"Katherine, that will be too difficult for the poor man. That is less than forty-eight hours away," Daniel protested.

Katherine gave him a speaking look before fixing a firm eye on the tailor. "You will be able to manage it, won't you, Mr. Wilson?"

"Of course, Miss St. Cloud. I will set all my people to work on it at once."

"Thank you, Mr. Wilson. I knew you would not fail me," Katherine assured him with a wide smile of gratitude. "My cousin is from the New World. He does not understand the Englishman's abilities."

Though Daniel wanted to protest, he knew it would prolong the session, so he stood silently with an intention to discuss Katherine's behavior with her later.

As soon as he was free of the tailor's measuring stick, he hurried off in the direction of the East Wing, where the estate manager kept his office.

"Don't forget Betsy Drake and Jack Burford will be here after lunch, Daniel. I will expect you to be finished with Cullum by then." Katherine smiled at his frown as he hurried away. Though she had been miffed at how Daniel had taken over, she was finding benefits to his management.

She retired to her room to choose her own apparel for the next evening's entertainment. Lady Priscilla was sure to wear one of her gowns from London, and she had no desire to be outshone by her hostess.

Having received acceptances from both Betsy and Jack, Katherine waited in the music room, with its pianoforte, for their arrival. She had every intention of using the afternoon not only to teach her cousin the dances but also to further the romance between her two friends.

Betsy's arrival first gave Katherine a chance to inform her of the treat in store.

"Jack is coming? Oh, no! I look a fright! I must redo my hair. And I'm sure my dress is smudged. Please, Katherine, take me upstairs at once," Betsy pleaded as she anxiously smoothed the skirts of her pink sprigged muslin gown.

The two young women hurried up the stairs, giggling as they went.

When Jack Burford was announced, Daniel was in the music room waiting to greet him.

"I appreciate your attendance, Mr. Burford. I do not want to embarrass my cousin by acting the country bumpkin tomorrow evening."

"I am pleased to be of assistance, my lord. But please,

call me Jack. Katherine and I have grown up together. It seems ridiculous to stand on formalities with her cousin."

"Thank you. My name is Daniel. Are you as familiar with Miss Elizabeth Drake?"

"Betsy? Lord, yes. We've all known each other since we took our first steps." The young man seemed at ease, a reminiscent smile on his face.

"Even Lady Priscilla?"

"No, not Lady Priscilla. Her family only moved to the area three years ago."

"Ah, that explains it." Daniel smiled charmingly at his neighbor.

"Explains what?" Jack asked as he was intended to do.

"The attraction Lady Priscilla has for the local lads."

Bewildered, Jack stared at his host. "You do not find her attractive?"

Daniel shrugged his shoulders. "She is somewhat pretty, though I find my cousin more so. But Lady Priscilla seems obsessed with her successes. A fellow looking for a wife would want someone interested in him, not just herself. Though I suppose I should not say so if I claim to be a gentleman." Daniel paused to let his comment sink in. "Take Miss Drake, for example. She is always ready to listen sympathetically. And she has the most charming sense of humor."

"I'm sure Lady Priscilla will grow out of her self-absorption. After all, she is very young."

Daniel shrugged his shoulders again. "You are probably right. I have found the best way to determine that is to look at the mother. Since I have never met Lady Crane or Mrs. Drake, I suppose I should reserve judgment."

Watching the thoughts flicker over the younger man's face, Daniel wondered if he had made any impression.

Just then the door opened to reveal the two young ladies.

Both men rose to their feet, Jack staring at Betsy in surprise. "I did not know you were coming, Betsy," he said.

"I asked Betsy to help us. I did not think you would want to dance with Daniel while I played the pianoforte," Katherine teased, with a sideways look at her friend. "And I thought you and Betsy might demonstrate each dance while I play before we teach it to Daniel. Then he can see how it ought to look."

"You do not mind, do you, Jack?" Betsy asked timidly.

"Of course not, Betsy. You dance admirably. It will be a pleasure," the young man said.

"That way both Betsy and I will enjoy dancing, instead of always being stuck at the pianoforte," Katherine added.

Everyone seemed in agreement, and Katherine motioned to Daniel to join her on the bench at the instrument. "You can turn the pages for me as well as watch the dancers, if you like, Daniel."

"Yes, ma'am," he agreed with mock solemnity, nothing loath to be in such close quarters with her. Katherine settled herself on the bench, intended for two players, and Daniel joined her there. She jumped in surprise, however, when his arm went around her waist.

"Daniel," she hissed, "what are you doing?"

"This is a small bench and I am a large man. You wouldn't want me to fall on the floor, would you?"

It was true that he took up all the rest of the bench, but Katherine knew her mother would not approve of such behavior. "Perhaps you had better stand, and I will turn the pages myself."

"Nonsense! I wouldn't hear of it."

Unwilling to make a scene, she yielded and tried to

ignore his warm hand on her waist. With a nod to the couple standing in the proper position in the center of the floor—Katherine had earlier had the Aubusson carpet rolled up—she began to play.

Jack and Betsy made a delightful couple as they moved about the room. The pair at the instrument watched them, only slightly distracted by each other's presence. When the song ended and the two dancers moved apart, Daniel rose from the bench. "Bravo. That was wonderful. Miss Drake, you are most graceful."

Betsy, with a smile on her flushed face, swept her friend's cousin an elegant curtsy. "Thank you, kind sir. I had a skilled partner."

"Pretty and modest to boot," Daniel murmured in Jack's ear.

"Any partner is skilled when paired with you, Betsy. You were always the best dancer among us," Jack assured his lifetime friend, determined not to be outdone by a newcomer.

"Enough compliments," Katherine insisted. "Now we must begin the difficult part, teaching Daniel the steps."

"Actually, this particular dance seems quite similar to one we dance in Montreal. Why don't we have Miss Drake play the music and let me see if I can adapt."

As Daniel swung her around the room in perfect time to the music, Katherine knew she had been misled. Not once did he make a misstep or show any hesitation. When Betsy finished playing the music, Katherine pulled away from her partner and put her hands on her hips. "You, sir, are a trickster!"

Daniel placed his hand on his heart and assumed a mournful pose. "Why, cousin, you have wounded me."

Betsy and Jack joined them. "That was well done, Lord St. Cloud," Betsy said with a grin.

"I think you may be able to give me pointers," Jack joked.

"I apologize to you, my friends," Katherine said. "I invited you under false pretenses, but I swear I knew nothing about my cousin's little joke."

"Nay, Katherine, I had no intention of teasing you. I did not know what dances you English might have devised that had not yet reached our distant shores. I was only trying to prepare myself for a brilliant introduction into society tomorrow."

"He's right, you know, Katherine," Betsy insisted. "We had better go over the other dances, just to be sure."

Since Katherine knew her friend did not want to miss any opportunity to have Jack to herself on the dance floor, she reluctantly agreed, though she cast Daniel a look promising retribution at a later date.

Katherine felt a growing excitement rising inside herself as the next evening approached. Her best gown had been refurbished with creamy French lace, and its pale gray silk for half-mourning shimmered as she moved.

With her golden curls elegantly piled à la grecque atop her patrician head, she swept down the stairs that evening, reminding Daniel once more of a heavenly being. Katherine had no complaint to make about Daniel's toilette either. His new clothes, a royal blue coat which needed no padding and a crisp white shirt, topped by a snowy cravat, only increased the man's attractiveness, Katherine thought with a sigh. As she reached the main hall, however, Katherine's eyes were caught by the large sapphire pin adorning Daniel's shirtfront.

"Where did you get that jewel?" she questioned sharply.

Daniel raised his eyebrows at her peremptoriness. "Is it not appropriate?"

"Of course it is!" she snapped. "But I never agreed to your dissipating the estate on such frippery."

"I have no need of your permission," Daniel said pleasantly, but with a touch of steel in his voice. "But do not fret, little cousin. This sapphire was a gift from a lady."

"A gift from a lady?" Katherine gasped. "And what did you do to earn such generosity?"

Katherine shivered at the flash of fire in his blue eyes, but when he finally spoke, there was only amusement in his tones. "I'm afraid I can't divulge that information, dear Kate. At least, not at the moment."

Daniel turned to run up the stairs to take her mother's arm in place of her maid and assist her to her daughter's side. Katherine watched his gallantry with misgiving. Daniel St. Cloud was so many different men, all of them fascinating, but few of them easily understood. And she knew nothing about him prior to his arrival here. He had revealed nothing of his past in any conversation, except the charade they had concocted at their first meeting.

She was about to dismiss thoughts of the man's past when something Jesse told her earlier in the day came back to mind. She had gone for a ride after breakfast. When she returned to the stables, Jesse himself had come to assist her from the saddle.

"Miss Katherine, I think I should tell you I heard something about Jem."

"Yes?" she responded sharply, swinging around to face the leathery old man.

"He went to America, like he always talked about."

Katherine frowned. "But I thought you said he needed money to do that."

"That's what bothers me, Miss Katherine. He was

seen in the village talking to a stranger. And Luke as has worked here most of his life says he saw the stranger give 'm a lot of money the day afore the Master's accident."

"Are you saying someone paid Jem to cause the accident?" Katherine demanded.

"No, Miss Katherine, I'm just saying it was a funny coincidence, like."

Katherine didn't like such a coincidence. "Have you spoken of this to Lord St. Cloud?"

"No, Miss Katherine. I didn't know whether to or not."

"I will speak to him about it. Does anyone know who the stranger was?"

"He hasn't been seen since. But he was a foreigner. He spoke like a Frenchie."

"I see," Katherine told the old man, even though she wasn't sure she did. She was rewarded with a look of relief. "Thank you for speaking to me, Jesse. If you hear anything else, please let me know."

Katherine had been distracted from her thoughts about Jesse's information, but it came back to her now as she watched her mother and Daniel approach.

"You speak French, of course, don't you, Daniel?" Somehow, though most of society spoke the language, there seemed to be a connection between the two strangers who had newly arrived in the area.

Her abrupt question caused her mother's eyebrows to raise, but Daniel showed no concern. "Of course I do. It is the common language in Montreal."

"But you said you were English . . . and you sound English."

"I am English. And all of Quebec Province is now English, but it was settled by Frenchmen and the language is still quite common there." He stared at her before adding, "But I had an English governess. Actually, she was from Scotland. That is why I call you my bonny Kate, which is certainly true this evening," he said, admiring her appearance again.

Ignoring his compliment, Katherine stared at him, wondering if he truly could speak French or if it was another part of the grand lie he was living.

Lady St. Cloud put an end to their conversation, insisting they be on their way before they were unconscionably late.

The Crane estate was halfway across the county from White Oaks. While the Cranes' house was large and decorated in the latest fashion, Katherine's father always said White Oaks was more elegant. Katherine agreed, but the big house did look imposing with the sun setting behind it.

They were the last guests to arrive, as everyone was eager to meet the newcomer in their midst. Daniel was already popular amongst the young people, and Katherine realized at once his impeccable manners would please the older element of the guests as well. Just as he had charmed her mother, so did he please the ladies he met, from Lady Crane to Mrs. Milhouse, the Reverend's wife. By the time dinner had ended and the men had joined the ladies, Katherine knew Daniel was a social success.

Lady Crane announced dancing for the young people if Mrs. Milhouse would not mind playing for them. After receiving that lady's cooperation, she approached her guest of honor with the offer of her daughter's hand for the first dance.

Katherine watched as Daniel led the elegant Lady Priscilla, shining in a blue tulle gown that she knew put her own gray to shame, out onto the floor. A young man

at his first evening party interrupted her thoughts to lead
her out, and Katherine caught only glimpses of the other
couple during the dance. But it occurred to her that her
plan was succeeding all too well. That thought caused
her to stop in the middle of the dance.

"Is anything the matter?" her eager swain inquired.

"Oh! No, I'm sorry. I—I forgot the steps for a
moment. Please forgive me." Her rosy cheeks only
added to Katherine's discomfort. She picked up the
dance steps and enslaved her partner with a brilliant
smile.

Though Lord St. Cloud partnered his hostess, as
courtesy commanded, his thoughts remained trained on
Katherine. His eyes narrowed as he caught a glimpse of
Katherine's smile and her partner's reaction. "Young
puppy!" he muttered under his breath.

Lady Priscilla, beaming as she felt sure all eyes were
on her and her partner, fluttered her lashes. "I vow, we
are so near the pianoforte, I did not hear your words,
Lord St. Cloud."

"I said it is a lovely party, Lady Priscilla," Daniel told
her, replacing his scowl with a pleasant smile.

"Yes, of course, though it cannot compare to the
parties I attended in London."

As the young lady droned on about her favorite
subject, Daniel was able to focus on Katherine once
more.

When the dance ended, Lord St. Cloud bowed over
her hand with grace, but before she could think of a
ladylike way to ensnare him for the second dance, he
gave way to the hovering Sir William.

After curtsying to her partner, Katherine looked up to
find Daniel looming before her.

"The next dance is mine, cousin," Daniel murmured in her ear. "I must take my turn before you enslave all these puppies."

Katherine's eyes rounded in surprise. "I do not take your meaning, sir."

As the music began, he wrapped his arm around her, pulling her closer than was the custom, whispering, "Yes, you do, my sweet."

All eyes were on the revolving couple. Most were admiring the picture of grace they made, their contrasting color and size complementing each other. Several observers, however, were not as pleased.

Lady Priscilla, watching the couple, realized this was the second time the gentleman of her choice had abandoned her in favor of his cousin. That thought did not please her.

Her partner shared her bitter feelings toward the couple. In addition to his desire for Katherine, Sir William deeply resented the brutal dismissal he had received from Lord St. Cloud.

While Jack Burford danced with Miss Drake, he mulled over his new neighbor's comments from the afternoon before. He had not abandoned his interest in Lady Priscilla, but Daniel's comments had somewhat eroded his infatuation. While Daniel might not know the mothers of the two young ladies, Jack did.

His partner was oblivious to the others. She knew that Jack would return to Lady Priscilla's crowd of admirers, but for the moment, he was hers.

"You look very nice this evening, Betsy," Jack said, realizing as he spoke that the civil words were sincere. Betsy's simple pink gown flattered her perfect complexion, and her chestnut hair was arranged in flattering curls.

Her cheeks grew pinker as she smiled. "Thank you, Jack, though I don't compare to your elegance. You are the most handsome man here," she finished in a rush.

Jack laughed. "You make me feel as though I were, even if it is not true, Betsy." He swung her closer to him in an elaborate step that delighted her.

By the end of the evening, Lady Priscilla promised herself she would never speak to Lord St. Cloud again, even while her eyes followed him across the room. He had danced the first dance with her and then had not approached her again, in spite of the numerous smiles she had sent his way. Even Jack Burford had not been as persistent in his pursuit of her. Instead, Sir William, who had been attendant upon Katherine in the past, had maintained a position near Priscilla all evening.

Katherine, the only woman with whom Daniel had danced twice, watched all evening to discover the young woman who had drawn his eye. Once they were in the carriage and Lady St. Cloud had drifted off into slumber, Katherine leaned forward to whisper, "Did you dance with the young woman who has caught your interest?"

Daniel smiled. "Yes, I did."

"Are you as attracted to her as earlier?" Katherine watched sharply in the moonlight for his reaction.

"More than ever, my Kate."

"If you would reveal her name to me, I could assist you in your courtship," Katherine promised, holding her breath for his response.

"Thank you, dear cousin," Daniel said with a knowing smile, "but I shall manage."

"Daniel!" Katherine protested, causing her mother to stir.

"Ssh! You'll awaken your mother. And she seemed exhausted by the end of the evening," Daniel commented, studying the older woman while she slept.

"I know," Katherine said with a frown, her mind distracted from his romance to more important matters. "I think I should send for Dr. Benjamin in the morning."

"As long as he does not want to look at *me*," Daniel said in distaste. "He wanted me to swallow the most vile concoction!"

"Poor Daniel," Katherine mocked with a chuckle. "That is a small price to pay for all you have gained by becoming my cousin."

"You are right, my Kate, but you have forgotten yourself again and you must pay the forfeit."

In truth, Katherine did not attempt to avoid his lips as they moved to hers. The warm caress fascinated her. A tentative hand reached up to touch the masculine cheek as Katherine submitted to his kiss. At her touch, his hands slid up her shoulders to caress her slim neck. As his lips parted from hers, Daniel whispered, "Ah, Kate . . ."

"Stand and deliver!"

The rough voice that intruded into their intimacy brought their carriage to an abrupt halt, almost throwing Daniel from his forward seat onto the ladies.

Muttering under his breath, Daniel righted himself and Katherine saw him searching for something in the darkness. "Daniel?" she questioned as she fingered the pearl necklace her father had given her on her eighteenth birthday.

"It will be all right, Katherine. Stay here with your mother."

Lady St. Cloud was struggling to come awake.

Katherine took her hands in hers. "Ssh, Mama. It will be all right," she said, unconsciously repeating Daniel's words.

"Everyone out of the coach," the rough voice commanded. Katherine obeyed Daniel's order to remain in the carriage, but she slid over next to the coach window as Daniel got out.

"You really don't want to disturb the ladies, do you?" Daniel asked coolly, after he had stepped out into the moonlight.

Katherine could see two figures on horseback, barely discernible in the shadows, though one was much closer to the coach than the other. The two men on the box, Jesse and one of the young stablehands, must not have been moving, because Katherine could hear nothing of them.

"I said everyone out!" was the gruff reply.

Daniel's steely reply cut through the night. "Take my advice, sir, and do not disturb my companions, or you will regret it."

Katherine shivered with fear as she heard the sound of a gun cocking. Her fingers squeezed her mother's hand tightly.

"You're foolhardy even for a swell!" the first highwayman exclaimed, and Katherine caught the gleam of his pistol in the moonlight. Silently, she urged Daniel to have care.

"I do not take kindly to being held up. However, I will offer you this sapphire pin if you will be on your way and disturb us no longer."

"That jewel and any others your companions are sporting will be mine anyway, my cocksure fellow, with or without your assistance. Now, open the door to the carriage and have your companions join us!"

Without warning, there was the roar of several gun-

shots, followed swiftly by the louder noise of a blunder-
buss. The horses shrieked, accompanied by Katherine's
frightened scream, immediately followed by the second
gunman's voice.

"*Merde!*" the man in the shadows screamed before he
and his horse disappeared into the dark forest.

Chapter Six

Amidst the noise of plunging horses, Katherine scrambled down from the carriage, only one thought in her mind. "Daniel? Daniel, where are you?" she moaned, her hands groping in the darkness. "Please, God, please . . . Daniel?"

There was a grunt and then a hoarse voice answered her. "Here, Katherine. I'm here. Be careful," he warned as she stumbled over his prone figure.

She crouched down beside him, and her fingers ran hungrily over his arms and shoulders, stopping along with her heart when she touched something sticky and wet. "Jesse? Are you there?"

"Yes, Miss Katherine. We'm both all right. I'm trying to get the horses under control," Jesse called over the noise of the four horses straining against the man's control.

"Tell whoever is with you to bring down the lantern. At once!" she commanded. "Daniel, you are injured. Please do not move," Oh, Lord, please let him be all right. Don't take Daniel from me too. Over and over she repeated that prayer as she waited for the lantern to come

78

down in the hands of the footman. When the flickering yellow light was shed on the man on the ground, Katherine held back another scream.

Blood poured from his left arm high up near his shoulder. Katherine drew her lace shawl from around her and, standing up, turned her back and lifted her skirt, ripping her cotton petticoat. Making a pad, she wrapped it around the wound and tied it into place with her shawl. Jesse calmed the horses and clambered down from the box. As Katherine finished her ministrations, he called from a distance.

"Miss Katherine, this one's dead."

"What?" Katherine asked distractedly as she drew Daniel's head onto her lap.

Jesse came back to the circle of light. "The Master shot one of them . . . well, he shot him dead."

"Oh, dear. What shall we do? We can't take the body in the carriage with us, and we must get Daniel back to the house and summon the doctor."

"We'll leave 'im here," Jesse said with practicality to the forefront. "The Master'll be all right, won't he?"

"Yes, of course. I'm sure he will," Katherine said, bending low over the still form. "Daniel? Daniel, are you awake?"

Roused from his semiconscious state, Daniel tried to sit up.

"Just a moment, Daniel. Willie and Jesse are going to help you into the carriage as soon as I can get in to hold you. You must help them all you can, Daniel, because you are a big man."

There was a grunt from the prone Daniel that Katherine hoped signified his comprehension. Sliding out from under her burden, she got to her feet, unmindful of the blood all over her skirt, and returned to the carriage.

"Mother? We must . . . Mother?" Even in the darkness, Katherine could determine her mother's state of unconsciousness. With a frantic look over her shoulder to see the men pulling Daniel to his feet, she pushed her mother's body aside enough to enter the carriage. Then she pulled her mother to the seat and felt for a pulse, as she had seen the doctor do. Though it was weak, she was relieved to feel a throb of life. But there was no time to revive her mother. She quickly made her comfortable as possible, covering her with the cloak the older lady wore outdoors even in summer, and sat back to receive her other patient just as the door opened.

Katherine leaned forward to ease the men's burden and steady Daniel and found herself almost flattened as he fell forward. The most reassuring sound since their evening had been so rudely interrupted was the throb of Daniel's heart on her breast. Using all her strength, she assisted him in sitting on the seat and held his head on her chest.

"I'm . . . too heavy," Daniel puffed, out of breath from his maneuvers.

"No, Daniel, you're fine. Don't move. We don't want any more bleeding than necessary."

"Your mother? I don't see Aunt Margaret." Concern for her mother despite his condition warmed Katherine's heart.

"She's fine, Daniel. I made her lie down to rest. She was upset."

Daniel subsided against her, and Katherine could not keep from stroking his cheek as his head rested against her heart. But the devastation only a few minutes had wrought made it impossible for her to think straight. Not only was Daniel injured, but also her mother was ill. A helpless feeling stole over her as the coach rocked along at a pace that seemed unconscionably slow.

* * *

A weary Katherine struggled to remain alert in a straight chair outside her mother's bedroom door. Doctor Benjamin had made a quick examination of Lady St. Cloud as soon as he arrived. After ordering the woman put to bed, he had turned his attention to Daniel.

In both instances, he had rejected Katherine's offer to assist him, choosing instead the placid Mrs. Greyson. He had muttered something about shock and made some order concerning herself, but Katherine had refused to cooperate. She would not seek her own bed until her loved ones were cared for.

Counting Daniel as a loved one gave her pause, but she knew he had long since attained that status. She had just refused to admit it.

After the doctor had attended to Daniel's wound, Katherine had slipped into his bedroom and placed a kiss on his pale forehead. Staring down at his sleeping body, she had recited the doctor's prognosis over and over again, almost as a chant. "A few days' rest and he will be as good as new."

Now, she awaited Dr. Benjamin's verdict on her mother. A cock's crow told her morning was fast approaching, and she wearily rubbed her eyes. The door beside her opened, almost throwing her from her chair by its suddenness.

Katherine jumped up, trying to read the doctor's face.

"You were supposed to be in bed," he said sternly as he studied her pale face.

"I must know how my mother is."

"Miss St. Cloud . . ." The doctor paused, unsure what to say. "Your mother's heart is weak. She is not in immediate danger, but . . . I can make no promises."

In spite of her efforts, the tears gathered in Katherine's eyes. "She . . . she will be all right. I know she will be all right. She just needs . . . a—a little time. That's all. She recovered after Papa died. She . . ."

The doctor caught her as she lost consciousness and called Mrs. Greyson to assist him in attending his third patient of that early morning.

When Katherine woke, it was to find her room in semi-darkness. She might have thought it still early morning had not her room faced the west, where a lingering rosy hue told of a sunset just past. She wondered why she would be in bed at that time of the day when the answer hit her. With a moan, she shoved back the cover and hurriedly rang the bell for Lucy.

Her maid had been waiting for her mistress's arousal in the dressing room. She entered the bedroom almost before Katherine's hand had left the rope pull. "Miss Katherine, how are you feeling?"

Katherine ignored the question and asked her own. "How is my mother? And has Daniel . . . Lord St. Cloud regained consciousness?"

"They have both woken sometimes. The Master has been running some fever. And the Mistress just lies there." Neither report brought joy to Katherine.

"Help me dress. I must see them at once."

"Now, Miss Katherine, settle down," Lucy said with the ease of a longtime servant. "Someone will be up here with some victuals for you in just a minute. You haven't eaten for almost twenty-four hours."

"I don't need food," Katherine snapped. "I need to see"—she fought back a sob—"Daniel and Mother."

"Now, Miss Katherine . . ." Lucy began in what she thought was a soothing voice, but it did not have that effect on her mistress.

"Never mind. I will go like this," she almost shouted,

wrapping her dressing gown tightly around her and striding from the room barefooted.

She went first to her mother's room. The gloomy stillness frighten her. Mrs. Greyson, sitting in the shadows, saw the young woman enter, but had no need to caution her for quietness. Katherine tiptoed across the floor to kneel by her mother's bed, her eyes fixed on the white face motionless on the pillow.

Laying her hand on the almost translucent one resting on the coverlet, Katherine whispered, "Mama? Mama, please get better. I—I need you, Mama." She lay her head down on those two hands joined together, and Mrs. Greyson rose from her chair to place her arms around the shaking shoulders.

"Come now, Miss Katherine, you mustn't cry so."

Katherine rose in answer to Mrs. Greyson unspoken command and accepted the invitation of the old woman's shoulder to receive her tears. After a moment, she raised her head, her chin high, and wiped her face. "I—I'm sorry, Mrs. Greyson. You must be tired also. I shall relieve you for a while. I can sit with Mama."

"I have only been here an hour or so, child. Her maid Flora was here most of the day. Have you had anything to eat?"

Katherine frowned in confusion. "Eat? I—no, I must see to my cousin."

"Child, you must not fret yourself ill. Lord St. Cloud is being well taken care of."

"I must see." The desperation in her voice convinced Mrs. Greyson that Katherine should be allowed to satisfy herself before her own needs were seen to. She followed the girl from her mother's room and found Lucy hovering in the hallway.

"Lucy, Miss Katherine is going to visit the Master,

and then she will eat something and allow you to tuck her back up."

"But . . . I must help with the sick ones. I—"

"Miss Katherine, this morning you fainted. The doctor left strict orders. If you do not regain your strength, it will be more difficult for us to care for the others." The confusion and fear on the young woman's face wrung Mrs. Greyson's heart, but she knew what had to be done. "You go visit your cousin and then you follow my directions. That's the best thing you can do to help your mother and cousin."

"Yes, Mrs. Greyson," Katherine said in a small voice. Lucy took her arm, as if she were an invalid, and led her to Daniel's door. With a knock, she advised Jacob that Katherine wanted to see her cousin. With a nod from Lucy, Jacob opened the door to Katherine and slipped from the room.

Alone with Daniel, Katherine knelt beside the bed and placed her hands on his fevered brow. Hot to the touch, his face seemed on fire. Katherine discovered the bowl with cool water and a cloth in it beside the bed. She squeezed out the cloth and rubbed its coolness across Daniel's forehead.

There was a comfort for Katherine in the cool caress of the cloth on Daniel's face. She rubbed his neck and, with great daring, even moved the cloth inside the top of his nightshirt. The bulge on his left arm that was the bandage drew her fascinated eyes. Even as she ministered to him, she again repeated to herself the doctor's prognosis.

"Katherine?" a thready voice asked, disturbing her concentration.

"Daniel? Daniel, how are you feeling?" she whispered.

"Katherine . . . Katherine . . . where are you?"

Finally understanding that Daniel was not fully conscious, Katherine laid her cheek against his. "I am here, Daniel, beside you."

Her boldness surprised her, but she dismissed such thoughts. Daniel was ill and she wanted him to be well. That was what mattered now.

"My Kate . . . I want my bonny Kate."

"I am always your Kate, Daniel." His restless calling disturbed her, and she sought some way to convince him of her presence. With only a slight hesitation, Katherine pressed her lips to Daniel's. His breathing quickened with her touch and Katherine held his cheeks in her soft hands.

A knock on the door alerted her to Jacob's entry, and she drew back from Daniel and again wiped his face with the cooling cloth.

Jacob came to the bed and examined his patient. "He seems to be resting easier, Miss Katherine. I think he was worried about you. He called out your name many a time."

"Yes," Katherine said simply. As she rose to her feet, she looked at Jacob. "You will call me if he becomes restless and needs me? I am not tired now. I slept all day. I could sit with him tonight," she offered eagerly.

"Nay, Miss Katherine, Greyson and I are taking turns staying with the Master. It's our duty," Jacob said with dignity.

Katherine was wise enough to know that Jacob saw his vigilance as his right, not only as his duty. With a sigh, she allowed herself to be led away by Lucy, who had entered behind Jacob. The maid popped her mistress back into bed and served her dinner on a tray. She wanted to feed Katherine herself, but her mistress refused coddling. In truth, Katherine had no intention of falling asleep again, as Lucy had insisted, but before she realized it, her eyes closed and she knew no more.

When next Katherine awoke, her room was light. Stirring, she recalled the events that had occurred the night of Lady Crane's party. She hurriedly slid from the big bed and rang the bellpull. While she waited for Lucy's arrival, she threw open the door of her armoire and selected a morning gown of blue muslin. Laying it out on the bed, she picked up a brush and, unbraiding her hair, pulled the brush through it with haste.

"Here, Miss Katherine, I'll do that," Lucy said upon entering the room.

"How are the others?" Katherine asked as she handed over the brush.

"The Master's fever broke early this morning. The doctor's already been to see him and says he's on the mend," Lucy reported with a smile.

Relief flooded Katherine and she collapsed on the seat in front of her vanity, her limbs shaky. "On the mend? Oh, thank you, Lord," she prayed. "And Mama?"

Lucy's smile vanished and she looked sympathetically at her mistress. "Lady St. Cloud is awful weak, Miss Katherine. The doctor looked at her, but . . . but he said there wasn't much he could do."

Katherine stiffened her spine and raised her chin. "Mama will make it. She is stronger than she looks. She just needs time, that's all. Has Cook prepared some of her good beef broth for her? Has the doctor said she may have some?"

"Yes, Miss Katherine," Lucy said soothingly. "Everything's being done for her."

"Good. Hurry with my hair. I must see Mama myself. She will be wondering where I am."

Nothing more was said between Katherine and her

maid. As soon as she was properly dressed, Katherine ran down the hall to her mother's room. Pausing outside the door, she drew a deep breath and pasted a bright smile on her face.

"Mama? How are you feeling today? " Katherine asked in soft, musical tones as she entered her mother's chamber, giving a brief smile to Flora, her mother's maid, who sat in faithful attendance.

The small woman moved her head slightly on the pillow and a faint smile appeared on her whitened features. "Katherine," she whispered weakly.

"My, you are looking much better today, Mama. I'm sorry you had such a fright the other night, but Daniel took care of us." Katherine's soothing tones held none of the terror she had experienced that night.

Lady St. Cloud watched her daughter with great intensity, but she made no attempt to talk.

"Daniel hasn't come to see you because he has had much to do, and he felt you might be embarrassed to have a man in your bedroom. I told him it would be better if he waited a few days.

"He is . . . all right?"

"Why, of course, Mama. He is fine. Have you been worrying about him? Shame on you. You know Daniel can take care of himself. And they got none of our jewels either. You must put it completely from your mind. Have you seen what a beautiful day it is? Flora? Would you pull the curtains open? Mama will love the bright day."

Katherine leaned over her frail mother and propped her up slightly as the maid did her bidding. As the light filled the room, chasing away the gloom, Lady St. Cloud seemed more alert. Katherine kept close watch on her mother's face as she gently chatted about commonplace things. She paused to ask Flora to fetch a tray for her mother and then continued her monologue.

By the time the maid had returned from the kitchen, Katherine had washed her mother's face and brushed her silver blond hair. "Here is some of Cook's famous broth for you, Mama. It will give you more strength," Katherine said cheerfully as she sat beside her mother, prepared to feed her.

After a few moments, Katherine wiped her mother's face again and settled her for a nap. She could force no more broth down her. "I think she will sleep for a while, Flora. Please call me if she needs me."

"Yes, miss," Flora sniffed. She did not like being denied the privilege of serving her mistress, even by Miss Katherine.

Heading for the next sickroom, Katherine restored her optimism and energy with deep breaths as she strode down the hall. She found less of either needed in Daniel's room.

"Good morning, Katherine."

"Daniel!" she exclaimed at being greeted by a much recovered young man. "You must feel much better! How is he doing, Jacob?"

"The doctor said he is a remarkably strong young man, Miss Katherine," his valet said with pride. "He will be up and about in a couple of days."

"If they would feed me anything but this wretched broth, I could be about my business today," Daniel complained, not happy to be ignored.

"Perhaps if you show a healthy appetite by eating all of it, I could convince Cook to prepare you a more substantial meal this evening."

"This evening?" Daniel asked in horror. "What about my noon meal? Surely I do not have to eat broth then also?"

Katherine could not hold back a laugh. It was such a relief to see him eager to be up and about. "Oh, Daniel,

I am so relieved. How would you like a nice omelet for your next meal?"

"I suppose that would do," he agreed grudgingly. He looked at his manservant. "Jacob, would you fetch me some ale?"

As soon as the servant left the room, Daniel asked, "Are you and your mother all right? You took no harm?"

"No, of course not. You protected us wonderfully well." Katherine smiled but avoided his eyes.

"Then why has your mother not been to see me?"

Katherine's eyes returned to Daniel's. She had not intended to tell him of her mother's collapse, but after seeing her this morning, Katherine knew her mother would not be visiting him for some time. "Mama . . . Mama is not well. She found the events distressing and the doctor has recommended she remain in bed for a few days."

"Is it anything serious?" Daniel's eyes searched Katherine's face.

She refused to admit the truth to that question even to herself. "No, of course not," she said cheerfully.

Daniel relaxed against the pillow. "Well, it was certainly a climactic end to our evening, was it not? Do you often have highwaymen in this area?"

"No, I have heard of none for years. Which reminds me, I must report the attack to someone."

"The squire said he is the local magistrate. I will send him a note when I am recovered."

"Oh, we must do something sooner than that," Katherine said as she frowned. "We cannot leave the body there. Good heavens, it has already been a day and a half. I will speak to Jesse as soon as I leave you."

Daniel reached out to catch her hand. "I do not like your dealing with such distressing events. Send Jesse to me and I will talk to him."

Katherine had dealt with many distressing details in the past year, but she had no intention of sharing that with Daniel, who, in spite of his brave words, was already looking weary from their conversation.

"You must save your strength for the next dancing party. You were a considerable success at the Cranes'. If you will only tell me the name of your beloved, I could inform her of your illness. She might then visit to ensure herself of your good health."

Her teasing had the gratifying effect of drawing a grin from Daniel. "You must not tease me, cousin. I am shy with females."

"Ha!" Katherine hooted. "I have never met a man less shy."

"Possibly, but then you have had almost no experience of men, my bonny Kate."

"Is your lady also shy?" Katherine asked casually, hoping her cousin would not notice her probing for information.

"One as pretty as she has no reason to be shy, but yes, I believe she is."

"Oh. She is pretty?" Katherine repeated, bothered by his praise of the unknown lady.

"Oh, yes. She is the most beautiful woman in the world," Daniel murmured, his eyes trained on his companion's face.

Frowning, Katherine said, "Then Lady Priscilla must be your lady, because she is accorded a diamond of the first water, even in London. You should have danced more than once with her if she is your choice."

With a rueful grin, Daniel said, "You must not take Lady Priscilla's opinion of herself as the gospel truth, my Kate. What a London dandy might consider beauty is not necessarily my idea of that elusive quality."

"Does that mean Lady Priscilla is not the one?" Katherine demanded, cutting through Daniel's explication.

"My determined Kate, I am feeling weary. Where is that rascal Jacob with my ale?"

Guilt colored Katherine's cheeks as she studied Daniel's face. "Of course. I am sorry to weary you." At that moment, Jacob returned with a large tankard for his master. Katherine watched as he drained it. "I will speak to Cook about an omelet, and if I receive a good report, I will try for a steak for your dinner. Will that satisfy you?"

"Very much so, my sweet cousin. But will you not come back to see me?"

"I will haunt your door, dear Daniel. You are not rid of me by any means," Katherine said with a warm smile.

"I never want to be rid of you, my dear Kate. Are you sure you came to no harm?"

"None at all. I am disgustingly healthy," she assured him before slipping her hand from his and leaving the room.

She walked downstairs and asked Greyson to send for Jesse. She did not want to think about the body of the dead highwayman, but something must be done.

When Jesse was shown into the Blue Salon, Katherine smiled briefly. "Thank you for your assistance the other night, Jesse."

" 'Tweren't nothing, Miss Katherine. It was the Master as was brave. I didn't fire until after he shot the first one. And I missed."

"But you kept the second man from returning fire. And you may have even hurt him. I believe he screamed," Katherine said, a vague memory stirring. Her concentration had all been on the fallen Daniel.

"Yes'm. He did. I was surprised."

"You were surprised that he screamed? I don't understand what you mean, Jesse," Katherine said with a frown.

"Didn't you notice, Miss Katherine? He spoke French."

Chapter Seven

Jesse's statement startled Katherine. "That was French? I had not realized . . . why would that . . . the foreigner!"

"Yes'm. That was the thought that crossed my mind. I haven't heard of no other foreigner in these parts. And it's kinda unusual to have highwaymen around here."

"Yes, it is, isn't it?" Katherine agreed while she frantically thought of the implications of Jesse's information. When she realized he was waiting for further instructions, Katherine pulled herself together. "We must do something about the body of the . . . the highwayman."

"I took some of the lads and a wagon and hauled the body over to Squire Burford. Mr. Greyson wrote a note explaining the events."

"You did?"

Jesse looked anxiously at his mistress. "We thought it was the thing to do, Miss Katherine."

"You are right, Jesse. It was perfect. Thank you for doing that. I was concerned about the—the body lying there in the woods." Katherine shuddered. "Was there . . . was there anything else we needed to do?"

"I don't rightly know, Miss Katherine. Squire Burford read the note and said he would call on you. And he said he hoped everyone recovered."

"Thank you, Jesse," Katherine said, patting the old man on the arm. "You have done exactly as you should, and I appreciate your help."

The old man's leathery skin deepened in its color. "It was nothing, Miss Katherine. We're all just glad those highwaymen didn't hurt you nor your mother."

After the old man returned to the stables, Katherine sat contemplating his information. She remembered looking out of the carriage and thinking that the second highwayman hung back in the shadows, as if observing the events but not participating in them. He must have known he would be easily identified as a foreigner if he spoke.

Even though they were close to the shipping channel to London, they had few foreigners in their village. Most headed at once to London rather than in the opposite direction, which only led to a small village. Why would this person have come to Whiteclif?

Even though she had avoided the thought, Katherine finally admitted there could be some connection between Daniel and the foreigner. They both spoke French. Was it possible the man, like Daniel, was from Montreal? Could an enemy have followed him from Canada? Of course, she could consider this to be a strange coincidence, but two serious accidents and the encounter with the highwaymen argued against it.

Katherine considered questioning Daniel, but in spite of his brave words, she feared he was still weak. She would go to the village and talk to Mr. Muncie, the proprietor of the Red Lion Inn in Whiteclif.

Relieved to have something to do, Katherine rapidly ascended the stairs and entered her room, where she found Lucy working. "I need my riding habit, Lucy."

"You are going out, miss?" the maid asked in surprise.

"Yes, I—I must talk to Squire Burford." She would swing back by his estate on the way home from the village. She didn't want anyone to know her movements.

"How is my mother?"

"She is still sleeping, Miss Katherine. Flora said your visit eased her considerably this morning. And making her take her broth helped."

"I will stop by her room before I leave. Tell Flora how much I appreciate her dedication to my mother's care," Katherine added. The maid had been with Lady St. Cloud since her marriage.

Once on the back of her favorite mount, Vixen, Katherine felt her cares slip momentarily away. The wind blowing her blond braid and the sun shining down upon her eased the building tension. Once she approached Whiteclif, however, her thoughts were forced back to more serious things.

"Miss Katherine," Mr. Muncie greeted her, coming out of his inn wiping his hands on his apron.

"Good day, Mr. Muncie," Katherine said as she dismounted.

"We heard about the highwayman. Is everyone all right?" the innkeeper asked at once.

"Yes, everyone is recovering nicely. May I have a glass of lemonade and one of your wife's delicious scones?" Katherine asked as she entered the inn. Her father had brought her here as a child to reward her for her horsemanship.

Mr. Muncie led her to the private parlor and scurried away to bring her her favorite treat. Serving the food and drink himself, he smiled as he set it down in front of the young lady.

"Mr. Muncie, before you go," Katherine said, halting the man's departure, "I need to ask you something."

"O' course, Miss Katherine."

"Have any Frenchmen stayed at the inn lately?"

"Why, yes, Miss Katherine. A man stopped here about a week ago. Right after Lord St. Cloud. He stayed almost a week. Leastways, I thought he was French, but you know, my wife is from Normandy, and she discovered he's from Canada—Quebec, he said."

"Did he mention Montreal?" Katherine asked, holding her breath.

"I don't rightly know, Miss Katherine. Would you like to talk to the missus?" the man offered, scratching his head.

"If she's not too busy, Mr. Muncie, please."

Katherine sat impatiently waiting for Mrs. Muncie. She had worked as a dresser to a London lady before she married Mr. Muncie, but she had soon settled to village life and was now accepted among the townspeople.

"Good day, Miss Katherine," Mrs. Muncie greeted her as she entered the room, her thin frame in contrast to her husband's burly shoulders. In a few minutes of conversation, Katherine learned that Mrs. Muncie had enjoyed the opportunity to speak French with the visitor but was disdainful of his crude accent. However, she explained, that was understandable since he had never seen France. His home was Montreal. She added he had not been seen in several days, though she understood he had visited her brother-in-law's butcher shop.

There was no other public accommodation in the area except Mr. Muncie's inn. Katherine tried one last question. "Did the foreigner meet any friends here? Or become particularly friendly with any of the local people?"

"No, I don't think so," Mrs. Muncie said, before

quickly adding, "Not that we keep a close eye on our guests. They are free to come and go as they please."

"Of course. Thank you for telling me about him. And should he come back, would you send word to me . . . without mentioning it to anyone?" Katherine asked pleasantly.

"Of course, Miss Katherine. Is anything wrong?" the dark woman asked, hoping for information she could share with her husband.

"Why, no, Mrs. Muncie. I was just curious." Katherine smiled her thanks but did not offer any coins for the information. It would offend Mr. Muncie. But she would order a lot of the bread Mrs. Muncie sold in the village. That would repay them for their assistance.

She left the inn and crossed the small, deserted street to the butcher's shop run by Mr. Muncie's brother.

"Good day, Miss St. Cloud," the man greeted her loudly, proud that others would see her enter his shop.

"Good day, Mr. Muncie. I wondered if I might purchase some of your special sausage. My cousin enjoyed it very much when Cook served it the other day." This attempt to gather facts was going to be costly.

"O' course, o' course. I'm glad it pleased Lord St. Cloud. How much did you want?"

Katherine asked for the least possible amount and watched as he prepared it. "By the way, Mrs. Muncie mentioned that the foreigner staying at their inn came in here yesterday."

"That's true." Mr. Muncie named off the man's various purchases.

Katherine listened intently. "Then he must not be returning to the inn."

The second Mr. Muncie paused, his lips pushed out in contemplation. "I guess you must be right. He didn't mention where he was staying now."

"Did he say he would return?" Katherine pressed.

"No, Miss St. Cloud, but I hope he does. The extra business is good for my own table," he assured her with a laugh.

Katherine looked around to be sure they were alone. "Mr. Muncie, I need your help."

"Why, o' course, Miss St. Cloud. What can I do?"

Katherine wished his voice did not boom against the walls of his shop. "Mr. Muncie, I need to know where to find this foreigner. If he comes in again, I would be obliged if you could discover where he is staying, and send word to me at once." The man nodded his head vigorously. "But you must tell no one about my interest."

"I understand, Miss St. Cloud," the man cheerfully agreed in his loud voice, leaving Katherine to wonder if he could keep anything secret.

Feeling there was nothing else to be gained from either of the Muncies, Katherine put her purchase in her saddlebag and remounted, turning her horse in the direction of Squire Burford's Manor.

Squire Burford's estate was west of the little village while White Oaks was south. Katherine galloped her mare through the woods that surrounded the village, suddenly aware of being alone. She had ridden the neighborhood most of her life, admittedly much of the time with a groom beside her, but sometimes alone, and it had never bothered her. Since their meeting with the highwaymen, however, she could no longer believe the woods were filled only with harmless animals.

When she arrived at the Manor, she headed straight to the stables and slid from her mare.

"Is anything wrong, Miss St. Cloud?" the stablehand asked, alarmed by the sight of the heated mare.

"No, no, not at all. Would you please walk Vixen? I

must see the squire." She walked hurriedly to the big house without waiting for his response, relieved to have arrived.

Squire Burford saw her at once in his library. Settling her on the couch, he resumed his seat in his favorite chair, his portly frame responsible for its sags. With a smile on his weathered face, an older version of Jack's honest features, he asked, "How are your mother and your cousin?"

"Much improved, Squire," Katherine said, hoping she was right. "I came to see if there was anything to be done about the highwaymen."

"It is highly unusual to have any in this neighborhood, my dear. I'm sure the one who escaped has gone away to more profitable areas."

Katherine debated how much to tell the squire. But in the absence of anyone in her own family in whom to confide, she said, "Sir, I think the highwayman who escaped was from Canada . . . like my cousin."

Squire Burford studied the young woman before him. He had known her all her life. He recognized fear in her words, and he sought to allay it. "My dear, there is nothing to fear. Such thieves are not brave men. I'm sure this one was frightened away."

"Squire Burford, you do not understand. I think . . . I think there is some connection between this man and my cousin."

"Surely you don't think Lord St. Cloud is in league with such thieves?" the squire asked in consternation.

"No! At least . . . I don't think so." Katherine faltered. "But there have been too many 'coincidences' lately. This is my cousin's third brush with death in a fortnight."

The squire was surprised and demanded an explanation. Katherine told him of the two previous accidents.

He rubbed his nose while Katherine awaited his reaction.

"Well, Katherine, I understand your concern. But all these incidents were such random events."

"The highwayman tried to kill him!" Katherine protested.

"Nonsense, my child. Highwaymen don't kill their victims . . . unless there is resistance, of course. Not that I blame your cousin for fighting them. But that is not their intention. You must not worry so. The dead thief was a local lad, a ne'er-do-well who has often caused difficulties. I am sure his co-conspirator is much the same."

Katherine grew more irritated. "Sir, I do not believe the other man was from England. I think . . . that is, I think this man is from North America . . . just as is my cousin. A man would not travel that far to be a highwayman."

"Of course not," Squire Burford said slowly, frowning. Then he smiled with relief. "He probably needed money to return to his homeland. That would explain it."

"No! It would not! Nor would it explain why he paid one of our servants to deliberately saddle my cousin's horse with an unmended saddle, resulting in an accident."

"Do you know he did such a thing?" the squire demanded, sitting up straight in his leather chair.

"I don't, for sure," Katherine admitted. "But everything points to such an action."

"Do you know of any reason why someone would try to kill your cousin?" Squire Burford asked.

"I think it is Sir William," Katherine said firmly, expressing the belief that had grown in her during the day, dismissing the Canadian in favor of a known enemy.

"Sir William? My dear child, Sir William is a gentleman. You cannot be serious."

"But he has always wanted our land. If my cousin dies without issue, it will revert to the Crown and he will be able to buy it." She paused and then added in a rush, "He proposed to me again, and my cousin sent him away with a flea in his ear. He was upset."

"I cannot believe Sir William would resort to such uncivilized behavior just because he wanted your land . . . or you. Not that you are not extremely attractive, child. As a matter of fact, his mother and I had hoped at one time that Jack would . . . well, that is neither here nor there."

"But won't some men do anything to get what they want?" Katherine asked, ignoring her host's last remark.

"Perhaps," the squire drawled, fingering his bottom lip as he thought. "But that does not explain the other man being from the same part of the world as your cousin, or the accident on board ship, does it?"

"I don't know," Katherine muttered. "I haven't been able to resolve those points. It seems impossible that it would be a coincidence, but . . ."

"Have you talked to your cousin? Perhaps something in his past would bring a clue."

Katherine shuddered at the thought. She was sure much in her "cousin's" past would provide clues, but she doubted it would shed any light on the recent events. "No . . . no, I have not. I will talk it over with him. Thank you for your time, sir."

"I am always glad to be of assistance, Katherine. But I must admit, I am relieved that your cousin arrived in time to claim the estate and care for you and your mother."

"I am also, Squire."

"You are fortunate, you know. Your time was running

out and he could have turned up too late. It can take months for a letter to reach Canada and twice as long to get a reply. I have heard cases where the heir arrived too late." Burford shook his head in amazement at such difficulties while Katherine stared at him in horror.

It had never occurred to her that her real cousin might still turn up to claim his inheritance. What would she do then? Would he expose their scheme? Katherine's mind whirled with this new possibility for disaster. With a shake of her head, she bid her host adieu and left his library just as Jack was running down the main stairs.

"Katherine! I did not know you had called."

"I needed to talk to your father," she said, smiling briefly at her friend.

"And you were going to leave without saying hello to me? I think I am offended," he said.

"Oh, Jack, you must not tease me. I have too many worries right now." Katherine noted her friend's elegant dress and unusual attention to his grooming, but her mind had too much to consider even to wonder why he was dressed so.

"I heard about your escapade the other night," he said, taking her arm to escort her to the stables. "Daniel is most courageous."

"Yes, he is. But his life is worth more than jewels . . . if that is what they wanted."

"What do you mean?" Jack demanded, pulling Katherine to a halt.

"What?" Katherine asked, unaware she had spoken aloud her thoughts.

"You questioned whether they wanted your jewels. What else would they be seeking?" Jack asked in confusion.

"Nothing. I didn't mean . . . I'm sure they wanted

our jewels." Katherine walked faster, anxious to escape
any more questions.

"Wait a minute, Katherine. What is your hurry?" Jack
asked, frowning.

"I—I must return home. Mother is not doing well, and
my cousin is still in bed with his gunshot wound. I don't
like to be gone too long."

"I had no idea your mother was ill. Was she injured?"

"No. No, but her heart is weak, and . . . and the
events of that night were distressing," Katherine said,
not slowing down.

"I'll ride with you partway," Jack offered.

That did slow Katherine's steps. "But are you not
riding over to Lady Priscilla's?" she asked in surprise,
his immaculate grooming making her assume that was
his destination. He frequented the Crane estate when
Lady Priscilla was not in London.

Jack's cheeks flamed and he look away. "Why, no,
not today. Betsy offered to help me with . . . my
French. She is quite a scholar, is Betsy. And . . . and
if I travel abroad, I would have need of French."

"Yes, of course, but I did not know you were
contemplating any travels," Katherine said, her eyes
trained on her old friend.

"Well, I am not, at least not at the present,
but . . . but it is best to be prepared."

"I quite agree," Katherine agreed, delight lifting her
anxiety for the moment. "And Betsy is a wonderful
teacher."

"Yes, she is, isn't she?" Jack eagerly agreed.

Katherine was distracted as she and Jack chatted about
their old friend while he rode alongside her. She rejoiced
in Betsy's good fortune, but her mind continued to stray
to her own difficulties.

As soon as the two parted company, Katherine set a

steady pace to reach her home. Next time she rode out, she would bring a groom with her. Her mother always insisted, but this time she had not wanted anyone to know of her movements.

"How is my mother?" was Katherine's first question upon encountering Greyson in the main hall.

"Resting comfortably, Miss Katherine, but she asked for you."

Katherine wasted no further time talking. Racing to her room in a most unladylike manner, she rang the bell sharply for Lucy and began pulling off her riding habit. Lucy arrived, and retreated immediately to bring the water Katherine needed for washing. She must not appear in her mother's room with the smell of the stable about her.

A short time later, Katherine raced down the hall dressed in a sprigged muslin gown, her blond hair braided down her back and tied with a matching yellow ribbon.

"Mama?" Katherine called in a soft voice as she entered the room. "How are you feeling after your nap?"

"Better, child, better." The weakness of her voice belied her words. "How are you managing?"

"Just fine, Mama. You know this house runs itself because of your fine training." Katherine leaned over to kiss her paper-thin cheek. "It is you who must be managed," Katherine teased. "You must eat more of Cook's good broth to restore your strength." With a nod to Flora, who brought over a neatly laid tray, Katherine helped her mother sit up slightly. "I have come to be sure you eat as you should. You bully poor Flora quite dreadfully, you know." Her warm smiled relieved some of the gloom of the room.

"She . . . is good to m-me," Mrs. St. Cloud said, finding speech difficult, a fact that alarmed Katherine.

Hiding her worry behind another smile, Katherine teased and prodded her mother into finishing almost half the bowl of broth Cook had provided.

Once she had settled her mother for another sleep, Katherine slipped from the room. In the hallway, her shoulders slumped and she bit her bottom lip to hold back the tears threatening to fall from her eyes. She went back down the stairs.

"Greyson, when was the doctor last here?"

The old retainer scratched his head. "Well, I believe it was about seven this morning, Miss Katherine. He was called to a laying-in and wanted to check on his patients here first."

"Who is having a baby?"

"Young Mrs. Brown over on the squire's estate. It's her first, so Doctor said it would take a while."

"I see." Katherine frowned before saying, "Could you send someone to the doctor's home with a request to come when it is convenient? I want to talk to him. If I am not present when he arrives, find me."

"Yes, Miss Katherine. Is everyone all right, miss?" Greyson asked with a worried frown.

"As well as can be expected," Katherine said, smiling to relieve his worry. "I'm going to visit my cousin now."

A knock on the door brought Jacob, a smile on his face. "Miss Katherine, the Master is much improved. Cook sent up the omelet you requested, and he liked it much better than the broth."

"I am glad, Jacob. I must speak to my cousin. May I come in?" Katherine asked when she realized the man was not going to open the door.

"He will be ready for your visit in just a few moments, Miss Katherine. I was helping him change his shirt when you knocked. Just a minute," he said as he closed the door.

Katherine stood in the hallway, irritated at being made to wait. She must discuss several things with Daniel, and none of them would be pleasant.

The door swung open and Jacob motioned her in with his hand. She discovered a pale but much recovered Daniel sitting up in his bed, a smile on his face.

"Welcome, cousin. I began to think you had abandoned me."

"Abandoned you?" Katherine asked in surprise. "I have only been gone a few hours."

"A few hours trapped in bed seems like days," he assured her with a grin. "This monster will not let me venture from my bed hardly at all," Daniel said, motioning toward Jacob, who grinned from ear to ear at his master's teasing.

"I should think not. You must be grateful he takes such care of you," Katherine responded, recognizing the rapport between the two. But what she had to say could not be discussed in front of Jacob, even though he knew the secret of Daniel's identity.

She gave Daniel a speaking look, trying to convey her need for privacy. "Is anything wrong, Katherine?" he asked.

"Why, no," she responded in frustration, "but there are several things we must discuss."

Comprehension lighted Daniel's eyes. "Jacob, would you go ask Cook for some tea? I am thirsty again. And Jacob," Daniel added as the manservant moved toward the door, "wait for the tray."

"But sir . . ."

"Jacob, there is no need to be concerned," Daniel said.

With a worried look at the young lady beside the bed, Jacob stood by the door, undecided.

"Trust me, Jacob. I will not betray you," Daniel murmured.

"Yes sir. I will return in fifteen minutes," Jacob promised.

"Your servant is loyal to you," Daniel said with a grin. "He fears I will ravish you if we are left alone."

"He does not realize your heart lies with another," Katherine said.

"It is not my heart he is concerned with," Daniel said wryly, ignoring Katherine's flush. "What is wrong?"

"Daniel, did you . . . that is, do you have any enemies?"

Daniel's eyes narrowed, never leaving Katherine's face. "Every man has enemies, Katherine. What do you mean?"

"I think one of the highwaymen was a Canadian, Daniel. From Quebec. And I believe the robbery the other evening was an attempt to kill you."

Chapter Eight

Daniel stared at Katherine and frowned as he contemplated her words. "Why?" he questioned.

"Do you not find it strangely coincidental that you have come close to death three times in the past few weeks?" she demanded.

Daniel's eyes flickered, but he said nothing.

"Well, I do!" Katherine insisted. "Besides, I have learned something about your riding accident." She explained about the damaged saddle and the missing stablehand.

"Why didn't you tell me this sooner?" he demanded.

"Jesse did not tell me until the day of Lady Priscilla's party, and I forgot in all the preparation. Since then, there has been no opportunity. Do you know who this man might be?"

"No. But if I had been warned, I could have looked for more information . . . or been better prepared," Daniel said thoughtfully.

"You did everything you could at the time of the robbery. You killed one of them."

"Yes, but the other hung back. Probably the Canadian?"

"Oh, yes, we're sure of it because he shouted something in French before he rode off," Katherine said, having suddenly remembered Jesse's revelation.

"What did he shout?"

"I'm not sure," Katherine said, pausing to remember what she had heard that night. "My French is not as good as it should be, but it sounded something like *merde*. It means nothing to me. Does it mean anything to you?"

Daniel grinned. "I'm glad it has no meaning for you, my sweet. It's not something a young lady should know. But it has no significance."

"I do not understand. Why is French not your first language if you are from Montreal?"

"In Montreal, you hear both French and English everywhere. My mother comes from an old French family, but both her husbands were Englishmen."

"How much of that is true and how much is made up to go with your new identity?" Katherine asked.

Daniel blinked and then said, "Remember, the best way to succeed at a venture like ours is to believe it is real yourself. Don't ask."

"That reminds me of something else the squire said that alarmed me. What if my real cousin should arrive here? Suppose the message hadn't reached him until now? It would take him a month or two to arrive. He could still turn up."

"I think it unlikely, Katherine," Daniel assured her. "And we have enough problems without inventing new ones."

"Perhaps you are right," she agreed with a sigh. "But what are we going to do? And why would anyone want to kill you? Do you have any idea?" Katherine asked, her eyes trained on his.

"No, Katherine, I don't," he replied emphatically,

"though it is clear you do not believe me. But I am going to get out of bed and find out."

"Well, you cannot get out of bed yet today. Besides, I rode to the village and asked around. This Canadian has not been seen for several days. He stayed at Mr. Muncie's inn almost a week, and Mrs. Muncie, who is French, says he is from Quebec."

"If you are not careful, word will get to him that you are interested in his whereabouts," Daniel warned.

"Of course I'm careful. I am not an idiot, you know."

"I think I should—" Daniel began as he raised himself up from his pillows.

"You will do no such thing. It is important that your wound not reopen. The doctor is coming again today, and you may ask him then if you can get up tomorrow. However, I don't think he will approve your riding just yet."

"Why is he coming again today? He saw me this morning," Daniel said.

Katherine's eyes clouded over. "It is Mama. I don't think she is doing well."

"But you told me it was nothing serious," Daniel reminded her.

"I know but . . . but I lied. Mama is not getting better. And . . . and Daniel, I am frightened," Katherine admitted, her voice shaking.

Daniel reached a strong brown hand to grasp Katherine's. "Is it her heart?"

"I don't know. The doctor said her heart was weak and . . . he said he couldn't promise me anything. When Papa died, Mama had to stay in bed for a while, but she recovered," Katherine assured him. "Surely she will this time too."

"We'll wait until the doctor comes. I'll talk to him, my Kate. We'll do the best we can for her."

Katherine squeezed his hand, grateful for the support. Her mother's illness frightened her. Except for her bogus cousin, she was alone in the world. And someone was trying to kill him.

Katherine found what remained of her day taken up by visits from her neighbors. She enjoyed the visit from Betsy, blooming in a rose muslin gown and escorted proudly by Jack. His presence kept them from discussing matters closest to Betsy's heart, but her friendship and support comforted Katherine.

Her next visitor was shown to the Blue Salon just as Betsy and Jack had risen to leave, and she looked none too pleased to see them in company. Katherine pleaded with her eyes for her friends not to abandon her, and they resumed their seats on the sofa. After greeting them, Lady Priscilla, in a plum merino walking dress topped by a straw bonnet with matching feathers, looked at the young man and said, "I had thought to see you this afternoon, Jack."

Such a pointed remark did not please him, and Mr. Burford shrugged his shoulders. "I knew Betsy wanted to visit Katherine to see if she had recovered from her ordeal, and I thought to lend her my escort."

"I too wanted to see if everyone had recovered. How is your cousin?" Lady Priscilla demanded, as she settled her skirts on the other sofa.

Mindful of the fact that this young lady could be the object of Daniel's affections, Katherine swallowed her dislike and murmured. "Much better, thank you. He may be allowed to leave his bed tomorrow."

"Ah. I shall return tomorrow then. If I had realized I would not be able to see him, I wouldn't have come today." Even Lady Priscilla recognized her remark as rude and hastily amended it. "Not, of course, that I do not enjoy visiting with you, dear Katherine, but my purpose was to assure Lord St. Cloud of my family's wish for his rapid recovery."

"I will be delighted to convey such a message to him and save you the trouble of traveling so far tomorrow," Katherine said with an overly sweet smile, knowing what her visitor's reply would be.

"But that would not be quite the same, would it, Katherine, dear?" Lady Priscilla smiled with gritted teeth. "Were it not absurd, one would think you jealous."

Katherine's cheeks flamed at the young woman's taunt, and Betsy, who had been silently watching what could only be called a confrontation, interrupted. "Since you are unable to see Lord St. Cloud today, Lady Priscilla, would you care to ride back with us? I'm sure after Jack has seen me home, he would be willing to escort you to your home."

Lady Priscilla would have been delighted had the offer come from Jack. But she did not want charity from someone so inconsequential in her scheme of things. She waited for Jack to offer himself, but that young gentleman seemed intent on studying the polish on his black boots. "That is most gracious of you," Lady Priscilla finally said, "but I must hurry home. I have to prepare for this evening. Sir William is joining us for dinner."

If she hoped to arouse any jealousy in the other young ladies by mentioning Sir William, she failed miserably. Katherine, as well as the other two, bid her good-bye. Once the door was closed behind her, Katherine burst out laughing. "Thank you, Betsy. I have never seen Prissy so effectively routed."

"But I was trying to be nice," Betsy protested even as she laughed.

"That was the most amusing part," Katherine assured

her. "She was horrified by the thought of being the recipient of charity."

"Well, she wouldn't have felt that way if Jack had spoken up," Betsy said, her questioning eyes on her escort.

"Why should I? You were the one who offered. I would have done as you asked, but it wouldn't be my choice."

"But I thought you . . ." Betsy began before realizing her words would be inappropriate.

Jack, however, ignored Katherine's presence. He had done a lot of thinking and observing, and even discussed his feelings with his father. The time spent with Betsy today had convinced him she would be the best mate for him. Even more startling, once he looked beyond the society glitter of Lady Priscilla, he found his heart in tune with his mind. "No longer. I have discovered the true meaning of love, Betsy."

Katherine held her breath as her two best friends stared at each other, entranced. When neither seemed to know what to say next, Katherine decided they should have privacy whether they wanted it or not. "I do not want to hurry you on your way, but Doctor Benjamin is returning to visit my mother and I must talk to him."

As if in a daze, the two rose and took their leave, but Katherine didn't think they even knew who she was. She watched them depart with happiness for them in her heart.

"The doctor has not yet come?" she asked Greyson after he closed the door behind her friends.

"He went up a few minutes ago, Miss Katherine."

Hurrying up the stairs, Katherine turned to her mother's room, hoping to find the doctor there. He was bending over his patient when she entered. "Doctor? I am glad you have come." She smiled down at her mother. "How are you, Mama? Aren't you glad now that I scolded you into taking Cook's broth?"

Lady St. Cloud made little response to her daughter's gentle teasing. To Katherine's eye, she seemed even smaller than her normal petite form, as if, little by little, she was slipping away.

Dr. Benjamin finished his examination and would have escorted Katherine from the room to discuss his findings, but Lady St. Cloud placed a frail hand on his arm. "I . . . I want—to know your diagnosis."

The doctor looked at Katherine and then his patient, undecided. Katherine saw the determination her mother's face and nodded in response to the doctor's unspoken question.

"Lady St. Cloud, you have experienced much tragedy in the last year. It has weakened your heart."

The frail woman nodded as if he had confirmed her own thoughts. "I do . . . not think I will recover," she whispered.

"I fear you may be right," Dr. Benjamin said reluctantly.

Katherine gasped, sinking her teeth deep into her bottom lip in an attempt to hold back the tears that flooded her eyes. Kneeling beside the bed, she clasped her mother's hand in hers and carried it to her lips. "Mama?"

"It is all right, child," Lady St. Cloud whispered. "I—I had already surmised . . . as much," she said breathlessly.

"I am sorry to have to give you such bad news, my lady. And I must remind you that I have been known to be wrong."

But both mother and daughter had recognized the seriousness of Lady St. Cloud's condition, though neither had spoken to the other about it. Now their eyes met in love and pain. They had supported each other through the difficult times that had fallen upon them. This time, Katherine would have to manage alone.

"I—I must . . . must see Daniel," Lady St. Cloud whispered.

"Mama, he is supposed to keep to his bed until tomorrow. I did not tell you earlier, but he was wounded by the highwayman."

"He will be all right?" her mother demanded with greater vigor than she had yet shown.

"He is a strong lad," the doctor said. "I believe he can arise from his bed and see you now, if that is your wish."

"Yes, please."

"I will bring him to you," the doctor said, and slipped from the room.

Katherine smoothed back a strand of silver blond hair from her mother's forehead and caressed her thin cheek. "Mama, is there anything I can do to make you more comfortable?"

"Yes, dear child, there is."

"Just tell me what it is, Mama, and I will do it instantly," Katherine promised with great fervor.

"I—I hope you will, child, but now is not the time to ask it of you."

"I don't understand, Mama. If you need something . . ."

The door opened to admit a pale Daniel and Dr. Benjamin, halting Katherine's words. Daniel hurried to Lady St. Cloud's bedside, taking her hand. "I did not know you were so seriously ill, Aunt Margaret. I am sorry."

"Thank you, Daniel." Lady St. Cloud looked at the doctor. "Pull a—chair to my bedside for Lord St. Cloud, and then escort my daughter downstairs. I must talk to him alone. I promise . . . I will not keep him from his bed for too long."

"But Mama . . ." Katherine protested in spite of a warning look from Daniel.

The doctor hastened to do her bidding. After seeing Daniel seated, he offered his arm to the younger lady. Katherine did not like what was happening, but with all three of the others in agreement, she had little choice.

Downstairs, the doctor offered to answer any questions Katherine might have about her mother's condition, but she could think of nothing to ask. "Please feel free to call me at any time, Miss St. Cloud, should you become concerned about your mother."

"Thank you, Doctor, and thank you for returning this evening. I know you must be tired."

"That is the life of a doctor, young lady, and I am content with it. By the way, your cousin is a strong young man. Do not be concerned about his health."

Katherine smiled a farewell to the doctor, thinking how much she had to worry about Daniel's health. As long as some stranger was attempting to rid the earth of Daniel St. Cloud, or whoever he really was, Daniel's health was most uncertain.

Her thoughts returned to her mother. She had saved the estate for her mother's sake, and now, after only a few days, her mother would no longer be there to share her life. Unconsciously, tears streamed down her face. She felt so alone. Only Daniel would remain of her family. But he really wasn't family, she reminded herself, however comforting it was to pretend.

She stumbled back up the stairs, unable to see through the curtain of tears, wanting to hide her sorrow in her room. She had to remain strong for the sake of . . . of whom? In the past, it had always been for her mother. Now, there was only the estate left. And Daniel.

Strong arms went around her, and Katherine knew instantly Daniel had found her. Leaning against that tall form, she found a comfort she desperately needed. "Oh, Daniel," she sobbed.

"I know, my Kate," he whispered, his arms holding her close. "Life has been hard for you these past several years."

"Mama . . . Mama is all I have left. It was for her that . . . that I did what I did," she said, caution checking her words.

"You have me, my bonny Kate. You will always have me," Daniel reminded her.

"But . . ." Katherine bit her lip again. She could not say that he really was not her cousin. And she could not mention the woman he loved. Not now. "Yes," she agreed, taking the solace she needed just now. She would be strong another time. "Yes, I have you."

Katherine spent a restless night. Several times she awakened and, drawing on her dressing gown, trod the darkened hall to her mother's room. The last time, just as dawn was breaking, she found her mother awake, lying alone in the darkness while Mrs. Greyson snored softly in the corner.

Kneeling by the bed, Katherine whispered, "Are you all right, Mama? Can I get you anything?"

"Nothing, my child," Lady St. Cloud whispered back, her breath light and ephemeral.

"I love you, Mama." Katherine's voice broke as she spoke, realization that this could be her last moment with her precious mother making speech impossible.

A cold hand stole to Katherine's face, cupping her cheek, and she turned her face into it, placing a kiss there. "My child," her mother whispered, "the time is near when I must insist that you obey me."

"You know I will, Mama. I—I want to do whatever will make you happy."

"You have always . . . made me happy, my darling ch-child. But you must not weep for me. I go to join your father . . . and Peter. They are waiting for me." There was a peace, a calm that steadied Katherine. If her mother was content, then she could be brave.

"There is only one th-thing left to do before I go," Lady St. Cloud whispered.

"What is it, Mama?"

"I will tell you later, child. But I want you to promise me. . . ." She paused to breathe. "Promise me you will marry Daniel . . . as we discussed."

"But, Mama," Katherine protested, "I cannot. . . ."

"Please, my . . . child. It is the only th-thing I ask of you."

Katherine pressed her eyes shut to hold back the tears that threatened to overwhelm her. How could she promise such a thing? Daniel loved someone else. So even if she gave her word . . . Her mother squeezed her hand, and Katherine was lost.

"All right, Mama, I promise to m-marry Daniel if . . . if he is agreeable," she whispered, licking her suddenly dry lips.

"Bless you, child," Lady St. Cloud murmured, closing her eyes. "Return to your bed now. We both must rest for what will come."

When next Katherine awoke, she found Lucy shaking her shoulder. "Miss Katherine, you need to dress at once. Your mother is calling for you."

"What? Is she . . . I'll come at once." Katherine swung out of bed and reached for her robe.

"No, Miss Katherine. The Mistress said for you to

wear this gown," Lucy protested, halting Katherine's progress.

She turned around to discover Lucy holding up a simple pale blue muslin trimmed in Valenciennes lace. She had had it made before her brother's death and had never had the opportunity to wear it. "But . . . but we are in mourning. It has only been a little more than six months since Papa . . . why?"

"I don't know, Miss Katherine, but those were her orders."

As unconventional as the request seemed, Katherine could hardly consider denying her dying mother anything, and so she allowed Lucy to help her dress. "Hurry, Lucy. I would never forgive myself if Mama . . . we must hurry."

Lucy assisted her mistress to don the gown, and then sat her down at the looking glass to brush her hair. "Hurry, Lucy," Katherine urged again.

"Your mama said I was to dress your hair with a blue ribbon in it, with ringlets, like you sometimes wear it in the evenings. I'm only doing what I was told to do."

Katherine fumed under Lucy's ministration. She was distracted, however, by the sound of a carriage arriving. "What time is it, Lucy?" she asked.

"It's almost ten o'clock of the morning, Miss Katherine."

"Who would be calling at such an hour?" she wondered aloud before fear gave her an answer. Her real cousin? Could her real cousin have appeared to claim his estate? Oh, dear God, please, I cannot bear such a thing now, with my mother on her death bed, Katherine silently prayed. "Lucy, discover who has arrived."

"But Miss Katherine . . ."

"Lucy, obey me," Katherine commanded harshly. The maid took one look at her mistress's determined face and dropped the brush she had been wielding. Katherine sat at tense attention, waiting for the maid's return. When Lucy slipped back into the room, she said, "Well?"

"It is the Burfords and Miss Elizabeth," Lucy said, her eyes wide with question. "They are waiting downstairs."

"But why . . . Hurry with my hair, Lucy. I must find out what is going on."

Lucy worked at top speed, finally threading the blue ribbon through her mistress's golden curls.

Katherine, normally polite to the servants, wasted no time on gratitude. She ran from the room down the hall to her mother's chamber. Without knocking, she burst into the room and found Daniel sitting beside the bed.

"Child," her mother whispered, but Katherine had no difficulty hearing her. She rushed to her side.

"Mama," she only said, bending to kiss the parchment cheek.

"You look beautiful," Lady St. Cloud whispered, reaching up to touch a curl as it lay on her daughter's creamy shoulder. "Does she not look beautiful, Daniel?"

"She is the most beautiful woman in the world, Aunt Margaret," Daniel said with a smile.

"Mama, can I get you anything? Why did you not wake me up earlier if you wanted to talk to me. I could've—"

"Hush, child. I did not want to awaken you until it was time."

"Oh, Mama . . ." Katherine moaned, tears in her eyes.

Reading her thoughts, Lady St. Cloud said, "No, child, I am not dying yet. Soon. But not yet."

Katherine looked at Daniel and then back down at her mother, a puzzled frown on her face. "Then why must I be dressed in a certain manner, and my hair done in this fashion? I do not understand, Mama."

"Do you remember this morning promising to obey me . . . to marry Daniel?" Lady St. Cloud asked, the struggle to speak causing beads of perspiration to break out on her forehead.

"Yes, of course, Mama, but you must save your strength," Katherine insisted, carefully avoiding Daniel's eyes. "You do not have to—"

"Yes—I must."

Katherine recognized that protests would only cause her mother further strain, and she waited for whatever her mother would ask.

"I—I want you to—to marry Daniel now." The whisper rang in the room as if it had been shouted.

Katherine stared at her mother and then turned to Daniel. He looked at her, his blue eyes serious, and nodded.

Katherine turned dazed eyes back to her mother. "Mama, you cannot know. . . ."

"Child, you . . ." She paused to cough, the struggle to talk becoming more and more difficult. "You p-promised." She closed her eyes in exhaustion and Katherine stared at her, at a loss.

Daniel stood up and reached over to take Lady St. Cloud's hand. "Aunt Margaret, let me talk to Katherine alone for a moment. Then everything will go as planned."

Without opening her eyes, Lady St. Cloud nodded, and Daniel helped Katherine stand and led her from the room.

In the hallway where Flora was hovering, Daniel motioned her into the room to care for her mistress, and he led Katherine to her mother's sitting room, closing the door behind them.

Katherine stared at him as if she had never seen him before. "What is going on?" she demanded.

"Your mother wants to be assured of your future, Katherine. It is important for her to know that you will be cared for after she is gone."

Staring up at the man who had taken over her life in only a few days, Katherine was speechless. Finally, she shook her head back and forth. "No, no, no, I cannot. . . ."

Daniel's eyes narrowed. "Will it be so bad, Katherine? I promise to care for you. I would never hurt you."

Katherine had no need of those reassurances. She had come to trust Daniel days before. But he loved someone else. He had told her so himself. And she felt sure that someone was Lady Priscilla. How could she marry him knowing he would always long for her neighbor. "I—I have taken care of myself for a long time now. This is not necessary."

"I'm afraid it is, darling Kate, if you want your mother to die peacefully. She doesn't have much longer."

Tears spurted into Katherine's eyes. She could not bear the thought of denying her mother a peaceful death but . . . "It would not be possible. We would need the vicar."

"Your mother has used her strength to obtain the necessary documents and has summoned Reverend Milhouse. She has even asked the Burfords and Miss Drake to attend." He reached out and took her hands as her cheeks paled. "Katherine, we could not live here together, once your mother is gone. It would not be . . . proper. Our relationship is too distant for society to accept it."

"But . . ." Katherine still protested, her mind unable

to function, only her heart telling her it would not be right.

"I will not force myself on you, Kátherine," Daniel said stiffly. "But you cannot deny your mother's final wish. This is for your mother, Katherine. You must agree to marry me now for your mother's sake."

His insistent voice pierced the daze that had frozen her thoughts. Her mother. Yes, she had promised her mother. Staring into his blue eyes, Katherine nodded. She was not capable of speaking.

Chapter Nine

Forever after, certain aspects of her wedding lived in Katherine's memory. The strange sight of many people crowded into her mother's bed chamber, the tight grip of Daniel's hand as he led her to her mother's side, the approving smile on her mother's wan face: All those things assumed an importance beyond their physical existence as she concentrated only on what she could comprehend.

"Katherine?" her mother whispered. "You w-will do . . . this for me?"

Her blue eyes dazed, Katherine stared at her mother. Nudged by Daniel, she whispered in turn, "Yes, Mama."

"Miss St. Cloud," Reverend Milhouse said, calling her attention to him. "Your mother has requested that I perform the ceremony, but I must have your word that this marriage is your desire."

Katherine slowly turned her head to the strong man beside her, a frantic question in her eyes. He returned her regard steadily, waiting for her response.

With a small sigh, Katherine nodded her head. "Yes Reverend Milhouse, I . . . will marry Daniel."

"Well, this is all highly irregular, but in the circumstances, I believe it is the proper thing to do." No one responded to his words, but Elizabeth moved forward to take one of Katherine's hands in hers.

Clinging to her friend's support, Katherine stood numbly waiting for someone to tell her what to do. It was Mrs. Burford who took charge. "Why do we not perform the ceremony here in front of the candles," she suggested briskly. "We want Margaret to have a full view of it. Flora, do you have the Book?" The maid, standing in the corner by the bed, keeping a jealous watch on her mistress, nodded, moving to the side table to take an ancient copy of the Book of Common Prayer and handing it to the vicar.

"Good. Now, Betsy, if you will stand beside Katherine, as her attendant, and Jack, you may be the best man, if Lord St. Cloud has no objection."

Jack eyed Daniel and received a grateful nod before taking the place his mother indicated. "All we need now is the ring and . . ." Since she was looking at Daniel, Mrs. Burford knew the answer before she finished her sentence. "You do not have a ring?"

"There wasn't time," Daniel admitted with a frown.

Lady St. Cloud interrupted. "I will not . . . need this anymore. It will give me great pleasure to know that my Katherine is wearing it." Her audience remained still, silenced by her struggle to remove the gold band from her finger, until Katherine fell to the bed, weeping, "Mama, Mama."

Again Mrs. Burford carried the day. Lifting Katherine from her mother's side, she comforted her as she would a small child, and then she told Daniel to assist Lady St. Cloud in removing the ring she had worn for so many years. Daniel, who wanted to comfort Katherine, followed Mrs. Burford's directions.

Wiping the weeping girl's pale face with her handkerchief, Mrs. Burford said, "Now, Katherine, I know this is difficult, but it is your mother's dearest wish that she see you married. If you want to make your mother happy, you must hold back those tears and allow Reverend Milhouse to begin."

Her sturdy practicality acted like cold water on Katherine's face. She straightened and stared straight ahead as the others grouped around her. With a nod from Mrs. Burford, the minister began the ceremony.

As one point in his lengthy discourse, Katherine's legs wobbled and she had a sensation of everything spinning. Daniel's strong arm came around her to pin her against his side, and she vaguely heard him urge the minister to be brief.

She remained aware of the goings-on to the point of responding when the minister requested her to do so, but she did not see the anxious faces around her. Only when the cold metal of her mother's wedding band was slid onto her finger did Katherine come back to reality. With a gasp, she stared at the gleaming circle of gold, and tears streamed silently down her face as she turned toward her mother, ignoring the pronouncement of her marriage.

Daniel's arm came around her to support her to her mother's bedside. Sinking down, Katherine kissed her mother's hand where the wedding ring had rested for so long. "Mama?" she whispered. "I love you, Mama."

"My—child," Lady St. Cloud whispered, closing her eyes as her soul departed.

Lady St. Cloud was buried in the family vault, next to her beloved husband. Katherine and Daniel, Lord and Lady St. Cloud, her only family, followed her casket to its resting place. The villagers and servants watched the young woman, swathed heavily in a black veil, lean on her new husband for support.

" 'Twas the best thing," they muttered among themselves about the hasty wedding. Miss Katherine needed someone to care for her, with all the difficulties she had faced in recent years.

Once the ordeal of the funeral was over, Katherine was dosed with laudanum and ordered to bed by Doctor Benjamin. "She has been pushed beyond her strength, sir," he told Daniel St. Cloud. "She must have complete rest if she is to recover."

"I agree, Doctor," Daniel told the man stiffly. "I can assure you my wife will be well cared for."

The doctor grunted and patted the young man on the shoulder. "You have many years yet to get on with life. Don't be impatient."

Daniel smiled grimly and ushered him from Katherine's bedroom, wondering if he and his wife would have the grace of those years. It was up to him to ensure that they did, he told himself, and he would do so. Katherine was his, and nothing would be allowed to come between them.

The doctor left more laudanum for Lucy to administer to Katherine when she came around, and it was several days before Daniel insisted the medicine be put away and Katherine allowed to awaken naturally.

When she first lifted her eyelids, there was nothing to remind Katherine of the many changes life had wrought. She was in her room, with its rose drapery, in her own comfortable bed. But her head felt as if it was stuffed with cotton, and her hand was shaky as she lifted it to push back her hair. The light reflected off the gold of the band on her left hand, and Katherine moaned as memories rushed in.

"Miss Katherine? Are you awake, miss?" Lucy demanded as she ran to the bed. Without waiting for an answer, she vigorously rang the bellpull.

"L-Lucy? My mother . . . she is gone, isn't she?"

"Lord love you, Miss Katherine, don't you remember burying her?" the maid asked in confusion.

Katherine closed her eyes as the pain washed over her just as her door was thrown open. Reluctantly, she opened them to see Daniel hurrying to her bed.

"Katherine?" he called softly, and tears suddenly streamed down her cheeks. Such tenderness made it impossible to be strong.

Without a word, Daniel dismissed the maid and slid onto the bed to gather his wife into his arms. He rocked her back and forth, crooning soft words that he was not even sure she heard as a torrent of sobs shook her. As he grew concerned that more laudanum would be required, Katherine's crying turned to silent tears that soaked his shirt.

He continued to hold her, stroking her back, smoothing her hair, his lips caressing her temples, until she lay spent against him. Then he eased her back against the pillow and got up.

"Daniel?" her scratchy voice demanded, afraid he would leave her.

Hearing the fear, he returned to her side at once. "I am only fetching a cloth to wipe your face for you, love. Do not worry. I am here."

Somewhere inside her was shame for her weakness, but need was stronger for the moment. Later, she would deal with such embarrassing cowardice. He returned to her side and placed the coolness of the cloth against her forehead.

Even as she faded from consciousness, exhausted by her mourning, she heard the deep voice beside her assuring her of his presence, his care. Cradled in his arms, she took refuge in sleep once more.

When Katherine next returned to consciousness, she was aware of everything that had happened. It was as if her bout of tears had washed clear her memory of the past few days. She lay still in her bed, her eyes wandering around the room, as various events played before her eyes.

The last of her family had died, and she was alone now except for her husband . . . who had wanted to marry someone else. Poor Daniel. Perhaps he would not think the bargain she had offered him was worth the price now. And then there was her own concern that she was married to a stranger with no knowledge of his past. What should she do?

With a sigh, she rolled over in the big bed. Her movement alerted Lucy, who hurried over to her. "Miss Katherine? Are you awake?"

"Yes . . . but don't call anyone," she hurriedly added as Lucy turned away.

"But the Master said to call him when you awoke."

"Lucy, look at me," Katherine commanded. "I am no longer distraught. I am going to get up now and dress. Afterwards, I will inform the Master myself of my state of health."

"Yes, miss," the maid said anxiously.

"Lay out—lay out a black gown for me."

"Oh, Miss Katherine, it's such a shame. Just as you was going into half-mourning and able to put away those awful black gowns."

"Yes. It's a shame," Katherine said in flat tones.

One look at her face and Lucy decided it would be best to work in silence. She assisted Katherine to dress, but made no comment when the gown fit loosely on her mistress.

"Just plait my hair and leave it down. I do not have the energy for an elaborate style today."

When she was ready, Katherine asked, "Is Lord St. Cloud keeping to his room, or has the doctor allowed him to come and go as he pleases?"

"Oh, he's almost completely recovered, Miss Katherine. Jacob says he's never known anyone recover as fast as the Master."

The pride his servants found in Daniel was amusing, Katherine thought, since he was an imposter. It was strange that even Jacob, who knew the truth, joined in boasting of Daniel's abilities.

Katherine met Greyson in the hall. "Miss Katherine? You are feeling better? Would you care for breakfast?"

"Thank you, Greyson, but luncheon will be in an hour, will it not?" At his nod, she said, "I'll just wait. I am not particularly hungry. Have you seen Lord St. Cloud?"

"I believe he's in the manager's office with Mr. Cullum. I'll inform him at once that you are up and about," Greyson assured her as he opened the door to the Blue Salon. "And I'll bring a tea tray at once."

In spite of her lack of hunger, tea sounded good, and Katherine smiled at his suggestion. "It is not necessary to disturb Lord St. Cloud. I'll see him at luncheon."

Greyson waited until his mistress was settled in the salon and then hurried down the hall to the small office in the East Wing.

"Sir," he said as he entered, "Miss Katherine is in the Blue Salon. She said not to disturb you, but . . ."

Daniel had arisen and passed the old man at the door before he could finish his sentence.

Katherine was seated at the pianoforte when Daniel

entered. She was not playing, but occasionally fingering a key, as if she intended to do so.

"Katherine, how are you feeling?" he demanded as he entered, his controlled energy awakening the slumbers of the room.

"Hello, Daniel. I am fine," she said, though her eyes fell away from his face almost immediately. "How is your arm?"

"Completely recovered," he assured her. He moved over to stand beside her and raised her chin. "You do not appear in your best frame."

"Thank you. I will come to you when I want someone to depress my pretensions."

Daniel pulled her up from the bench and led her over to a blue damask sofa. "You are always beautiful, my bonny Kate, but you are pale, and you have lost too much weight."

"I will eat a big dinner," Katherine suggested nonchalantly. When Daniel made no response, she eyed him from the corner of her eye. "What have you been doing?"

"Discussing the estate with Cullum. He is a good man."

"My father always found him so," Katherine said. "Have you discovered anything about the Canadian?"

"No. He has probably moved on to richer areas."

Katherine turned and studied her husband's face, her discomfort overcome by her curiosity. "You truly believe that?"

When he didn't respond, she said, "You don't believe that. You are saying what you think will satisfy me."

"I don't know," Daniel admitted. "I have seen nothing of him, and as far as I can discover, neither has anyone else."

"I see." Katherine waited for Daniel to say more, but he made no attempt to initiate conversation.

"I—I appreciate your support while . . . at my mother's funeral . . . and after." She was mortified by her behavior, but she felt it would be cowardly to not offer her appreciation.

"It was a difficult time, Katherine. I am glad I was able to assist you."

"Enough!" Katherine snapped, springing from the sofa to stride across the room.

Daniel sat still, watching in silence as his bride released her pent-up anguish. Finally, he asked calmly, "Enough of what, Katherine?"

She turned to face him, her jaw squared, her blue eyes fierce. "Enough of your best manners. You are in a despicable situation, and I suspect you would like to kill me!"

"Why would you think that?"

"Because you have been landed with a wife who has cried all over you and left everything up to you, when you had already chosen someone else to be your bride."

Daniel rose and walked over to her. Katherine wanted to back away, but she would not let herself do so. "You are the strangest female," he said lightly. "You are embarrassed by your tears, are you not?"

Katherine turned away. "No . . . not by my tears," she whispered. "They were for my mother. But . . . I should not have collapsed, like a weakling. I am responsible for . . . for everything here. I should have shouldered my duties."

"Katherine . . ." Daniel protested but halted when the door to the parlor opened to admit Greyson with the tea tray. Katherine returned to the sofa, unwilling to allow the servants to observe her disarray.

Daniel sat down beside her and pretended they had not

been interrupted in an emotional discussion. "Thank you," he murmured to Katherine as she handed him a cup of steaming tea, while Greyson looked on, beaming. Catching the butler's eyes, Daniel motioned for him to depart.

Before Katherine could erupt again, Daniel took matters into his own hands. "Katherine, everyone has moments of weakness. I hated being in bed with my wound, but I followed directions from the doctor. You were ordered to bed by the doctor and you followed his orders, as you should have. That is all there is to it, and I want to hear no more about your weaknesses. Otherwise, I would have to admit to mine."

Katherine's eyes widened in appreciation of her husband's understanding. When he finished, she nodded, saying, "Thank you."

"Good. Do you feel like a short ride to blow away the cobwebs before luncheon?"

Grateful for such a distraction, Katherine nodded.

"Go change into your habit. I'll tell Greyson to delay the meal for half an hour." He watched her hurry from the room. He would have to be alert for fatigue. She had been in bed for several days. But Daniel hoped to distract her from the anguish she felt in having failed in her duties. He had never known a woman with such a sense of duty.

Katherine breathed deeply. Summer in England was a marvelous thing, she decided. Turning to her companion, she asked, "Is summer in Montreal as wonderful as this?"

"Yes, I think so, my Kate. We have more sunshine around Montreal in the summer. But our winters are more severe."

"Really? Tell me about them."

"We have a lot of snow. For several winters, I lived in the wilderness with trappers, learning their trade. I thought I would never be warm again."

"You lived with trappers? Why?"

Daniel maneuvered his horse closer to his wife's. "Well, I thought I could learn a lot by doing so."

"Did you?" Katherine asked, her interest caught.

"Oh, yes. I learned to care for myself. One does not take a valet into the wilderness. And I learned I could survive without the most basic comforts."

"Were you successful at trapping?"

"Successful? I believe so," Daniel said, a secret smile on his face.

After a moment, Katherine said, "There is so much I do not know about you."

"You may ask me anything, my Kate."

"Daniel, what are we going to do about our marriage?" she blurted out, asking the one question that had been on her mind ever since she awoke.

Daniel reached out to her horse's reins and pulled both mounts to a halt. "What do you mean, Katherine?"

"Daniel, I know you were . . . interested in someone else. I would not have forced you into this marriage if there had been any other way, but . . . I feel terrible about it."

Daniel did not respond and urged the horses into a walk. Katherine waited for some kind of answer, but none seemed to be forthcoming.

"Daniel?"

Without looking at her, Daniel said, "I have no regrets about our marriage. Be patient, Katherine. Everything will work out."

Katherine was troubled by his answer. He was hiding something from her, and she felt sure it was unhappiness over his situation. She did not blame him. But she wished he would be honest with her.

"Come on, Kate. I will race you to the stables," Daniel suggested suddenly. As he leaned forward over his horse to urge him into a run, there was an explosion of sound. Katherine was stunned. It was the sound of a gun, but who could be hunting on her land?

Daniel felt the shot whistle past him just over his lowered shoulder and realized they were the targets. He pulled his horse to a halt, but knew he could not pursue his attacker until Katherine was safe. "Fast, Katherine! Race to the stables!"

Finally grasping what had happened, Katherine spurred her mare, shouting, "Hurry, Daniel!"

Together they raced across the meadow, heads low over their horses' necks. When they pulled up in the stableyard, several stablehands rushed up to take their horses. "Kate, go straight to the house and remain there," Daniel ordered in a voice to be obeyed. But he reckoned without his new bride.

"Not unless you come with me," she insisted, her voice shaking.

"I am going to find out who fired that shot."

"No! Jesse will take some boys and see what they can find. You are not to offer whoever it is another target."

When he appeared unyielding, Katherine, for the first time in her life, resorted to feminine wiles. She grasped his wrist, tears filling her eyes, and pleaded. "Daniel, please. I cannot live without you."

Jesse, who had listened to their conversation, agreed with his mistress. "Where was it, Miss Katherine?" he demanded urgently, having already ordered several horses saddled.

"On the far side of the meadow, where the north

woods begin," she snapped. "And, Jesse, take weapons."

"If you find anyone, I want him brought back here. I would know just why someone is shooting at me," Daniel added. As Jesse and his men mounted and rode from the yard, Daniel turned back to his wife. "I think you just took advantage of me, my Kate."

"What do you mean?" Katherine asked, her blue eyes wide.

Daniel dismounted to stand beside his wife. Leaning forward, he held her chin while his lips covered hers. When he released her, he muttered, "It was either that or a spanking, Lady St. Cloud."

Katherine said nothing, but she had no complaint about his choice.

Chapter Ten

Once they were in the house, Katherine relaxed slightly. At least here Daniel was not in danger. Greyson, unaware of anything unusual, announced luncheon.

Exchanging glances with her husband, Katherine, afraid to let Daniel out of her sight, signaled they would go into the dining room at once.

Both Daniel and Katherine avoided conversation while Greyson or the other servants were in the room. It was impossible to make idle conversation while their minds were on the recent attack. When they were alone, Katherine asked, "Do you think they will find him?"

"No. Too much time will have passed."

The harshness of his tones disturbed her. "You are angry with me because I did not let you return to search?"

Daniel stirred his fork in his food, his eyes lowered. "Of course not."

Angered by his obvious lie, Katherine retaliated. "You should be grateful that I wanted to keep you alive."

"Since you lose the estate if I die, it is no surprise that you are concerned," he pointed out wryly.

136

"You think . . . of course, how silly of me to think you would not remember," she ground out.

"I did not mean—" Daniel began when Greyson reentered the room.

The butler raised his eyebrows when he realized neither plate had been touched. Daniel interrupted his departure. "You might as well take this with you, Greyson. I'm afraid Lady St. Cloud and I have little appetite today."

"Yes, sir. I'll bring the next course. It's a nice piece of sole with lemon sauce. One of your favorites, my lord."

Silence was maintained while the servants removed one course and brought in the next. Katherine regretted the harsh words they had exchanged. As soon as Greyson and his footmen left them alone again, she said, "Daniel, I am sorry. I should not have lost my temper. I—I do not want anything to happen to you because . . . because you are the only family I have left. I . . . of course I care about what happens to you. I never thought of the estate."

"I was upset also, Katherine," Daniel said gravely. "I should not have said such a thing. Let us forget it." When she made no move to touch her sole, Daniel reminded her, "Greyson is expecting us to at least taste this course, or I'm afraid Cook will resign."

"Yes, of course," Katherine agreed, picking up her fork, all the time wondering whether her shaking hands would allow any of the fish to reach her mouth.

After a moment of silence, she burst out, as if she could not hold back her words any longer, "Daniel, do you have no idea who could want you dead?"

"I swear, Katherine, in spite of your vivid imagination concerning my past, I can think of no one who would be interested in seeing me dead."

Frowning as she stared at her husband, Katherine said, "Then it must be Sir William."

"What?" Daniel demanded in surprise.

"I said it must be Sir William. He has been after our land for several years. And—and he wanted to marry me. You treated him harshly when he came here to discuss it. Perhaps he is seeking revenge as well as the land."

"I cannot believe I upset him to the extent that he would have me murdered," Daniel protested.

"You are forgetting the land. Before you arrived, I heard he had made an arrangement with the Crown to purchase the land as soon as we had forfeited it. With you dead, there is no question but that it would go to the Crown."

Daniel's eyes narrowed. "You're correct, Katherine, but I still cannot—"

"Daniel!" she protested indignantly. "This is possibly the fourth attempt on your life. And Sir William seems to be the only person with a wish to see you dead." She paused as another thought struck her. "You have not dallied with any married ladies, have you?"

"That will be enough, madam," her husband said sternly. "We'll leave any past romances out of this. You must just take my word for it that there are no enraged husbands lurking in the woods to wreak revenge on me."

"Then we are left with Sir William."

"I find it difficult to credit, but I will ride over and discuss it with Squire Burford this afternoon."

"No!" Katherine insisted as Greyson entered the room.

"I beg your pardon, my lady?"

"No, I was not speaking to you, Greyson," Katherine said hurriedly.

Greyson stared down at their plates. "The fish was not

to your liking? Cook was sure she prepared it the same way you praised last week."

Katherine saw Daniel's embarrassment and decided openness might serve best rather than offend Cook. "Greyson, someone tried to kill Lord St. Cloud while we were out riding and we . . . Greyson!" she cried out as the old man paled and wavered on his feet.

Daniel jumped up to steady him, pulling out an empty chair and forcing the butler to sit. Katherine poured a glass of brandy from the sideboard and brought it to Daniel. Taking it, he offered it to Greyson, who gratefully accepted it. As he set the glass on the table, the butler realized he was seated while those he served were hovering over him. Jumping up, he stammered an apology.

"Nonsense, Greyson," Daniel replied, patting the old man on his back. "We are sorry to startle you. My wife did not want Cook to think we do not appreciate her wonderful cooking. And you would have heard it sooner or later."

"But my lord, who can be doing such a terrible thing?"

"That is a question we have not been able to answer."

Once Greyson recovered and left the room, Katherine had no difficulty remembering the train of their conversation. "You must not ride to the squire's place this afternoon. I will go, or we will send a note asking him to come here."

"Katherine, I will not cower inside this house the rest of my life, afraid to go about my normal pursuits," Daniel insisted, outraged at such an idea.

"And I will not have you blithely offer yourself as target practice for anyone!"

Their eyes engaged in a duel, with Daniel's finally falling. He reluctantly recognized the wisdom in her words. "All right, I'll write the squire a note asking him to call."

"Thank you, Daniel," Katherine said softly with no note of triumph in her words. She had been fighting for his life, not to win an argument.

"I believe you should return to your bed after you have finished eating," Daniel added, his eyes noting the exhaustion evident on her face.

"I will gladly do so if you will promise not to venture out and to awaken me when the squire arrives. I want to be there with you."

Daniel saw the stubbornness he was coming to know and agreed to her terms. With some semblance of a plan, they nibbled at the food before them. Greyson's entry ended that activity.

"My lord, Jesse has returned."

"Send him in at once, Greyson." Daniel stood up, anxious to discover his news, as the head stableman entered. "Did you find anything?"

"We didn't find the man, but we found where he waited for you to ride by. And we found where he'd been staying," Jesse said, justifiably proud of his work.

"Where?"

"There's an abandoned hut not far from there, near the spring. We trailed him back to it. There were signs someone had been there recently. The fire was still fresh." He shook his head in disgust. "We tried to follow a trail from the hut, but there were too many, all going in different directions. Looks like he'd been there for days."

Chills went down Katherine's spine at the thought of a murderer lurking so near to her home. Her eyes met Daniel's and he nodded. "Good job, Jesse."

"Yes, sir." The man paused as he started to leave.

"My lord, we'll keep watch, but you'd best stay low right now."

With a rueful smile, Daniel admitted, "You and Lady St. Cloud have the same idea, it seems. I will follow your advice for the moment, Jesse, but I have no intention of hiding forever."

Jesse nodded at Katherine and then turned and left the room. Daniel looked at his new bride. "Have you finished eating?" he asked gently.

"Yes, I—I have lost my appetite."

"You haven't had one for days, my Kate. I'm afraid you will make people think I am starving you."

His attempt at humor brought no relief to Katherine's fears, but she smiled dutifully. "I will assure them of your devoted care. You—you have been all I could ask for, Daniel."

"I was not seeking a compliment, my love, but thank you just the same. It has been a pleasure to serve you. Come, I'll walk you to your room."

Taking her hand, Daniel escorted Katherine up the stairs to the door of her bedroom. With a light kiss on her cheek he turned to go, only to find a small hand holding his coat lapel.

"You will keep your word, Daniel? You will remain in the house?"

"I promise, Katherine. I am only going downstairs to write a note to the squire. After that, I will work on the accounts. A very safe way to spend the afternoon, I assure you."

"And you will awaken me as soon as the squire arrives?"

"Immediately."

Satisfied, Katherine reached up and kissed Daniel on the mouth and then slipped into her room before he could react. He stood staring at the door before walking back down the stairs, a small smile on his lips.

Katherine fell into a deep slumber, and Lucy had a difficult time of it when the Master sent word for her to be awakened. Groggily, Katherine sat up, and Lucy had to repeat her message several times before it pierced Katherine's daze.

"The squire is here?"

"Yes, Miss Katherine, I mean, my lady. That's what I been telling you."

Katherine dressed hurriedly and raced down the stairs, bursting into the parlor before Greyson could even open the door for her.

"Good day, Katherine," Squire Burford said, rising as she entered. His son followed suit, and Daniel walked over to take his wife's hand and lead her to the sofa alongside himself.

"I have just been informing the squire of our mishap this afternoon."

"Most unfortunate," Burford said, shaking his head.

"It was not an accident, Squire. It was a deliberate attempt to kill my husband," Katherine protested.

"I did not mean the attempt was an accident, Katherine. Only that it was unfortunate that such a thing should occur when you and Lord St. Cloud have just been married."

"Did you not see anything?" Jack asked.

"No, we did not. I could not stay and search because I wanted to ensure Katherine's safety," Daniel explained.

"Of course," Burford agreed. "That was the best thing. He may have had a second gun at the ready."

"Did you tell the squire what I suspect?" Katherine demanded.

"No, not yet," Daniel said, uncomfortable with an unfounded accusation.

"It has to be Sir William," Katherine said. "Daniel can think of no one from his past, and Sir William is the only one with a reason to attack him."

"But Katherine . . . surely you do not think a gentleman would . . . well, it is just not to be considered," the squire protested.

"Neither is the death of my husband to be considered," Katherine replied coldly, fed up with protestations of gentlemanly behavior while someone was trying to kill Daniel.

"She has a point, Father," Jack said, siding with his friend. "At least it would not hurt to talk to Sir William."

"You want me to walk into a man's home and accuse him of attempted murder?" the squire asked, irritated.

When neither young man responded, Katherine said, "I will be happy to do so!"

Daniel caught his rebellious wife's chin between his fingers and said with a slight smile, "You will remain at home."

"No, Daniel! You cannot leave me behind!"

"Katherine, this is men's work. Sir William will be offended enough if our accusations are false, but to accuse him before a woman, and one to whose hand he had aspired, would be an incredible insult."

"Aye," the squire seconded. "That would be most improper, Katherine. You'd best let us men handle this."

"But you will confront him?" Katherine persisted.

The three men looked at each other, and finally Jack said, "We will do everything we can to bring this nightmare to an end, Katherine. You must just trust us to do our best."

"And . . . and you will not let any harm come to

Daniel?" Katherine demanded, her eyes fixed on her husband's face.

"Katherine!" he protested. "I am able to take care of myself."

Ignoring his remark, Katherine turned pleading eyes on the other two.

"We will leave our mounts here and travel to Sir William's home in a closed carriage, with several outriders," Squire Burford said. "He will be safe, Katherine."

"Thank you."

Daniel was embarrassed by his wife's demands, and his voice was quite cool as he suggested they depart at once. Katherine knew he was displeased with her, but his safety was more important than his pleasure at the moment.

After the men's departure, Katherine was at a loss as to how to fill her time. She was not sleepy, and she had never been interested in needlework, much to her mother's dismay. She was debating the attraction of a book or work on the household accounts when Greyson announced Elizabeth Drake.

"Betsy!" Katherine greeted her warmly. "I am so glad you have arrived. I desperately need a diversion just now."

"Then I am pleased to provide one, I wanted to see how you did after such a difficult time." Betsy sat down beside her friend, taking one of her hands in hers.

"It—it was not easy, but Daniel was all that was kind. This is my first day out of bed, actually," Katherine admitted.

"You have had to withstand so much this last year. If I may be of assistance, Katherine, you know I would do anything for you."

"Thank you, Betsy, but truly, there is nothing. Except keeping me company until Daniel returns."

"With pleasure. Where has he gone?"

Katherine jumped up from her chair to stride about the room. "They have gone to visit Sir William."

"They?" Betsy asked, her curiosity aroused. "I did not think Daniel and Sir William were friends."

"They are not. And Daniel is accompanied by the squire and Jack."

"Oh. Then I shall be doubly pleased to keep you company until their return. I had hoped Jack would call on me this afternoon. When he did not arrive, I'm afraid I left in a fit of pique," Betsy confessed with red cheeks.

"It is not Jack's fault," Katherine assured her friend. "Something occurred that made . . . that is . . . oh, you might as well know. Someone fired a shot at Daniel as we were out riding."

"No! Good heavens, was he hurt?" Betsy demanded urgently.

"No, thank goodness. But that is the fourth time someone has tried to harm him. I just could not bear it if . . ." Katherine broke off, unable to voice her fears.

"But what are they going to do about it? And why have they gone to . . . do they think it was Sir William?" Betsy demanded.

"No, they do not, but I do. I convinced them they must at least confront him with the events. He wants this land, Betsy, and if Daniel dies, he can purchase it from the Crown."

"Unless Daniel leaves an heir."

Katherine turned and stared at her friend. "There is no possibility of that . . . yet." She ignored Betsy's surprised look and added, "Anyway, I don't want anything to happen to Daniel."

"Of course not. That is barbaric. I'm sure Jack and his

father will be able to assist Daniel. You'll see, Katherine. Everything will be all right."

"I hope so," Katherine whispered, returning to sit beside her friend on the sofa.

Betsy decided diversion would best serve her friend. "Everyone was quite surprised about your marriage." When Katherine looked at her sharply, she added, "But they approved of your mother's action. All, that is, except the Cranes." With a giggle, Betsy continued, "The servants say Lady Priscilla was beside herself with rage when she heard about it."

Instead of amusing her friend, Betsy was dismayed to discover Katherine distraught. "Katherine, whatever have I said to upset you?"

"Oh, Betsy, it is terrible. I had to go ahead with the marriage, but I knew . . . Daniel . . . my plan backfired."

"Heavens, Katherine, what are you talking about?" Betsy demanded, putting an arm around her friend.

"Mama talked to me about marrying Daniel right after he arrived and . . . and I didn't want to think about marriage. So I had the picnic to introduce Daniel to other women. You remember. I discussed it with you."

"Well, yes, of course, but—"

"My plan worked too well," Katherine said, as a lonely tear traced a path down her white face. "He said he found someone who attracted him. I—I teased him about who it might be, but he would never tell me. But he said he danced with her at the Cranes' party and she was the prettiest one there."

"You mean Prissy?" Betsy asked, horrified.

"I don't know! I asked if it was she, but he made some riddle about people having different opinions about beauty. All I know is, he fell in love with someone and then was forced into marrying me."

Betsy studied her friend's tragic countenance. "Oh, Katherine, surely . . . I'm sure he will come to love you in time. You are such a wonderful person . . . and quite beautiful, you know. I have always thought you more beautiful than Lady Priscilla, in spite of her London gowns and town airs."

Hugging her friend, Katherine gave a teary chuckle. "You would say so even if I had spots, Betsy."

"Probably, but you do not have spots. Have—have you talked to Daniel about this?"

"I tried once, but he refused to discuss it," Katherine said, shaking her head. "Since then, all our discussions have been about whoever is trying to k-kill him." She buried her face in her hands. "I don't know what to do, Betsy."

"I think you are doing all you can, Katherine. And if you give Daniel time, I believe he will be happy married to you."

"I hope he has time," she whispered. "I . . . Oh, thank you, Greyson," Katherine said as the butler entered with a tea tray. "Pardon my manners, Betsy. I forgot to offer you tea."

"My goodness, has Cook learned to make rolls like Mrs. Muncie?" Betsy demanded as she examined the offerings.

"Like Mrs. Muncie?" Katherine asked, surprised. She swung around to stare at Greyson.

He cleared his throat. "Mr. Muncie brought them and asked me to give you this note, Miss Katherine."

With a gasp Katherine reached out for the piece of grubby foolscap folded several times. "Thank you, Greyson. Is he waiting for an answer?" she asked as her fingers itched to open the paper.

"No, my lady. He said he had to return to the inn."

"Then, thank you, Greyson. That will be all."

As soon as the butler left the room, Katherine unfolded the paper, muttering, "Excuse me, Betsy."

Her friend sat patiently watching Katherine scan the note and then reread it. Finally Betsy prodded, "What is it? Are you conducting a secret affair with Mr. Muncie?"

Katherine stared past Betsy, scarcely seeing her. "No," she replied absentmindedly. "I beg your pardon, Betsy, but I must leave."

"Katherine! Where are you going? What was in the note?"

"Mr. Muncie's brother saw the Canadian. He came to his shop today. I must go talk to him."

"Well, I am not going to let you go alone. I will accompany you," Betsy said sturdily.

"All right, but we must hurry. I'll ask Jesse and another of the stablehands to ride with us," Katherine planned.

"Just to the village? Do you think that is necessary?" Betsy asked in surprise.

"Daniel was attacked in our north meadow, Betsy. I had always considered it safe, but no longer. And I won't give Daniel the chance to complain about my behavior. Not now."

Soon the two young ladies and their escort were galloping down the narrow cart path to the village. When Katherine and Betsy entered the butcher shop, however, they tried to behave as if they were only interested in the sausages Mr. Muncie sold there.

"Good day, ladies," Mr. Muncie greeted them before turning back to serve his other customer. "Here ye be, Freddy. You tell your mum that's my best cut of meat."

The young boy gave the butcher a toothy grin and the two ladies a bow and ran out of the shop. Since they were now alone, Katherine wasted no time.

"Your brother's note said the Canadian came in today. What time would that be?"

"My lady, he strolled in here as bold as brass about two o'clock. I was that surprised to see him. I thought we'd seen the last of him. Word is he might be one of the highwaymen who shot Lord St. Cloud."

"Possibly."

"Well, anyways," Mr. Muncie said, trying to hide his disappointment that the young lady had not given him a more interesting response, "I asked him where he was staying, careful-like, you know."

"And did he tell you?" Katherine asked impatiently.

"No, my lady. He mumbled something about staying with friends. And I said, 'What friends might that be, 'cause I know most everyone in these parts?' But he didn't answer me. He just bought a lot of supplies, like he wouldn't be back for a long time."

Katherine stood waiting, but Mr. Muncie just grinned at her. "Is that all? Do you not know in what direction he left?"

"Why, no, my lady."

After closing her eyes in frustration, Katherine gave Mr. Muncie a tight smile. "Thank you for alerting me to his appearance, Mr. Muncie." She opened her reticule and took out half a crown. "This is for your troubles."

"Aw, Miss Katherine, this really isn't necessary," the man said as he pocketed her money. "I'm always glad to be of service, you know."

"And I appreciate it," Katherine said, backing out of the shop before she felt forced to buy something. She had expended a great deal of effort for little information.

On their horses headed back to White Oaks, Betsy asked, "Did his information help any?"

"Not really," Katherine said with a sigh. "Except that

the man is highly intelligent. After shooting at Daniel, he knew we would be searching the woods. And I'm sure he realized it would not be wise to reappear in the next few days. Now he has enough supplies to hide in comfort."

"Oh. Then perhaps Daniel and Jack and the squire discovered something."

"I hope so," Katherine said. Her strenuous first day out of bed was taking its toll. When the house came into sight, Katherine suggested they stop at the front door and let the grooms lead the horses back to the stable.

Betsy examined her friend. Exhaustion was clear on her face. "That's a good idea."

After giving the grooms those instructions, the two young women dismounted and turned to enter the house. Just as they reached the door, it was swung open and an enraged Daniel shouted, "Where the devil have you been?"

Chapter Eleven

Stunned, Katherine stared up at her husband and then at the squire, Jack, and Greyson in the background. "What's wrong?"

"What's wrong?" Daniel repeated as he grasped her shoulders and shook her. "What's wrong? We are chasing a murderer and you disappear? Can you not understand what is wrong?"

"I did not disappear!" Katherine insisted as soon as he stopped shaking her. "We went to the village in response to Mr. Muncie's note from the inn." She looked over his shoulder. "Didn't you tell them about the note, Greyson?"

The old man blanched. "I—I forgot, my lady."

"Probably because *someone* was yelling," she said, giving Daniel a speaking look.

"Katherine is really quite tired," Betsy said, speaking up for the first time. "Perhaps we could continue our discussion in the parlor?"

Daniel took a good look at his wife's face and scooped her up in his arms. "Thank you, Miss Drake. Please, won't you join us?" He stepped back to allow her to precede him. Jack took Betsy's arm.

"Daniel, put me down," Katherine whispered indignantly. "I am perfectly able to walk."

"Be quiet. I am debating whether to send you straight up to bed."

"You may be master of White Oaks," Katherine said stiffly, "but you are not master over me."

"I have wedding vows that say differently, Lady St. Cloud, or have you forgotten that already?" Daniel asked mockingly.

Since that was exactly what had happened, Katherine had nothing to say. Daniel strode past Greyson holding open the door, ordering a tea tray as he did so, and deposited his wife on the sofa.

"Now, tell us about the note from Mr. Muncie."

"I had visited Mr. Muncie's brother, the butcher, earlier, asking him to inform me if the Canadian returned to his shop. Today, about an hour after someone shot at you, Daniel, that same man appeared in his shop and bought enough supplies to last for several weeks."

"If Mr. Muncie said that in his note, why did you go to the village?" Jack asked.

"He did not say that in his note. He wrote only, 'The foreigner came to my brother's shop.' I thought I might be able to learn more." Katherine glared at the gentlemen. "Especially since I had been excluded from your activity."

The three men shared exasperated looks. "Was there anything else his brother could tell you?" Jack asked.

"No. Nothing. It was a wasted trip."

"And a dangerous one," Daniel added.

"Betsy, you must not ride alone anymore until this is settled," Jack ordered the young woman sitting beside him.

"Of course, I would not. And Katherine wisely had several men accompany us." She turned to Daniel. "She said she knew you would be alarmed if we went alone."

Daniel smiled first at Betsy and then Katherine, trying to make up for his earlier temper. "That was wise of you, Katherine. I'm sorry I was angered, but I was afraid something had happened to you."

"Did you not inquire at the stables? They could certainly have informed you of my whereabouts," Katherine said coolly, not yet ready to forgive.

"We hadn't got that far. I just assumed you would be here waiting for us. And when Greyson said he did not know where you had gone, I'm afraid I . . . I'm not a terribly patient man." Concern for her safety was visible in his face and Katherine capitulated, reaching out her hand to take his.

"Well, I think Jack and I should ride around the neighborhood and alert everyone of the stranger in our midst. While his attacks seem directed at you, my lord, we don't want anyone to take chances," the squire said.

"Did you talk to Sir William?" Katherine demanded.

"Yes, but he had nothing to do with the attacks on Daniel," Jack assured her.

"How do you know?"

"Because he was dumbfounded by our accusations," Daniel confessed with a chuckle. "In fact, I thought he was going to pass out when he realized what we were saying."

"He could have been pretending," Katherine stubbornly insisted.

"Katherine," the squire said in a firm voice, "Sir William may want your land. He may even have wanted you. But the man doesn't have enough backbone to kill a rabbit."

With a sigh, Katherine slumped back against the sofa. "But—but he was our only suspect. What do we do now?"

"Daniel will have to be very careful . . . and stay home as much as possible. And Daniel, you should direct the care of the estate from indoors. Your own land was proven unsafe for you today," Jack reminded him.

"I also intend to search for this man. He must be hiding somewhere in the area. I want to know why he is trying to kill me."

"Daniel, that will be so dangerous. Please . . ." Katherine pleaded with large eyes.

Daniel stared down into her face before turning to his guests. "I thank you for your assistance today. If you will excuse me, I think I should escort Katherine to her bed. I'll return in a moment to serve the tea Greyson is bringing."

The other three immediately voiced a need to return to their homes. Jack added that he intended to escort Betsy home first. Katherine protested their going, assuring them her husband was wrong, but everyone could see just how tired she was. When they had departed, Daniel wasted no time in picking up Katherine and heading for the stairs.

"Daniel, I am so embarrassed. You practically threw our guests out."

"That is not true, my Kate. I simply excused us. I did promise to return, you know."

"But I am not that tired. Truly. Just . . . just a little."

Daniel pressed a kiss on her forehead. "You were not supposed to overdo things your first day out of bed."

Finding his arms a most comfortable way to travel, Katherine said, "But I am not the least bit sleepy, Daniel. Only a little tired."

"I will have Greyson serve your dinner on a tray after you are tucked up."

"But I would rather dine with you," Katherine

pleaded, looking up at his face from beneath her lush lashes.

"Well, I thought you might allow me to join you, since I do not care to dine alone either," Daniel confessed.

Snuggling her face into his neck, quite content, Katherine murmured, "With pleasure."

Dressed in her nightgown and robe, Katherine leaned back against the numerous pillows. She was replete from her meal. Daniel had pulled a chair and table over beside the bed and they had enjoyed a most intimate dinner for two. In spite of the recent events, Katherine felt more at ease than she had in several years.

"Thank you, Daniel," she murmured.

"For what, my Kate?"

"For taking care of me, for making me forget all the horrible things that have happened, for . . . for being you."

"I find it a most pleasurable thing to be me when I am in your company. I am glad it pleases you," Daniel said with a smile. "Especially since you have many years of me to look forward to."

For the first time that evening, a frown crossed Katherine's forehead. Unwilling to spoil the evening, she remained silent.

"What is it, Katherine?"

"Nothing," she hastily said.

"You must not think about that man. He will not be allowed to destroy what we have," Daniel said firmly.

"I believe you," she said with a smile, extending her hand to his. His warm strength flowed to Katherine, sending her heart racing.

"It wasn't that, was it?" said Daniel. "Something else caused that frown. What was it?"

"Daniel, you must not try to read my mind," Katherine protested. "That would not be a good quality in a husband."

"Kate," was all he said, but Katherine could hear the stubborn persistance that meant he would not let his question die.

Turning her face away from him, she murmured, "I was thinking back to the picnic. Do you remember it?"

"Most vividly. Why?"

"You told me afterwards that there was someone there who interested you. And you told me you danced with her at the Cranes' party. Someone to whom you were . . . were attracted." Katherine swung back around to face her husband. "You never told me who she was, but I think I know."

"Do you?"

"Yes, yes, I do. And that is why I felt so badly about marrying you." She leaned forward, tears in her eyes. "But Daniel, truly, I had no choice. I could not deny my mother the comfort she sought in knowing I would be cared for. But I feel so guilty for having denied you your chance at happiness."

His blue eyes studied her wan face before he said, "You must not worry about that, Katherine. I have no complaints about our marriage."

"But there might be some way to set it aside as long as we have not . . . that is . . ." Her cheeks suffused with color as she tried to explain her meaning.

"I have no desire to set it aside."

Katherine stared at him, but he turned away, hiding his thoughts. She reached out and plucked at his sleeves. "Daniel?"

"What?

"You—you will abide by our marriage vows?"

He swung back around to face her. "Katherine, you are my wife and will be my wife until the day we die, and that is all there is to it." The fierceness of his words surprised her.

There was silence, and he again refused to meet her eyes. She laid her hand on his arm, feeling the iron strength of it through his coat. "I owe you a great deal, Daniel," she whispered. "And I want you to be happy."

"You owe me nothing!" he almost shouted, jumping up from his chair and striding over to the window to stare outside.

Katherine did not understand his strange mood, unless he was regretting his decision to become Master of White Oaks. So much had happened since then. But as Daniel had pointed out, it was fruitless to worry about the past. "So . . . what do we do now?" she asked.

"We find the man who is trying to kill me. Then we'll see."

She wanted him to return to his chair. He was too far away from her. "Do you think the person is trying to kill you because you are the heir to White Oaks?"

"I do not know. There must be some reason. And nothing like this happened to me before I came here."

"Except when you were knocked overboard. You knew nothing about the estate then," Katherine reminded him. She frowned as she saw Daniel's start of surprise. "Did you forget about that?"

"Yes, yes, I forgot. That was such a long time ago." He seated himself again and reached out to take her hand. "Before I met you seems a different life."

"I hope that's good."

His smile sent tremors of warmth through Katherine's veins and she clung to his hand. Though she was inexperienced in the ways of lovers, Katherine knew only the man before her could satisfy her heart. But if his heart belonged to another, would he willingly come to her bed? Perhaps . . . if to do so might save his life.

Her thoughts recalled her earlier discussions with her mother and Betsy about an heir. But her concern lay with Daniel, not the estate, or even herself. Even though he was an imposter, he was now her husband, and she clung to him.

A daring plan began to unfold in her mind, one that might stave off attacks on Daniel and convince him to consummate their marriage at the same time. Just as she had acted to save the estate, Katherine felt it was up to her to save Daniel. Her plan was not perfect, but it might buy them some time. The only question was did she have enough nerve to carry it out.

She peeped up at the handsome man near her, and her love for him gave her courage. He would think her too bold, and it might give him a disgust of her, but she had to try something.

"Daniel . . . Daniel, if we are to be man and wife . . ." She paused, unsure how to explain her thoughts to Daniel without embarrassing herself. "I mean, perhaps, as Mama said, the first thing we should do, before we worry about your killer, is to secure the inheritance." Her hand trembled in his as she waited anxiously for his response.

"What do you mean?" Daniel asked, staring at her.

"If—if you do not find me repugnant . . ." She flashed a look at him, afraid of what she would read in his eyes. "And we are married . . . we should. . . ."

Katherine breathed a sigh of relief that she did not have to say anymore for Daniel to understand her. With great gentleness, he said, "I have never found you repugnant, my bonny Kate, but you have . . . that is, these past few days have not been easy for you. I think it would be best if we waited until you have fully recovered."

Katherine shielded her eyes with her lashes. From his

first kiss, she had become more and more entranced with Daniel's touch. She did not want to wait anymore to discover the secrets of marriage.

"I am fully recovered, Daniel," she said firmly, bringing her eyes back to his face.

"The doctor said you should have complete rest for at least a week."

"He said the same thing about you when you were wounded. Did you listen to him then?"

"That's different, Katherine."

"I do not see why. And if our having a son will lessen the threat to your life, I think we should consider it."

Daniel frowned, even as his thumb caressed her palm. "I would not want to leave you with child, alone in the world, should something happen. And, besides, there is no guarantee our child would be a boy. If I were not here to protect you and you had the additional burden of a child . . ."

The pain his words brought caused Katherine to tighten her hold on his hand. She wanted to say that carrying his child would give her a reason to live should he be taken from her, that she wanted to be as close as possible to him, to know every ounce of his being. But that would be saying too much to a man who'd been forced to marry her. She sought reasons to convince him. "Daniel, if I am with child when . . . if anything should happen to you, they could not take White Oaks from me until the babe is born, at least."

"I see," he said, with a grimness that concerned her. "So you want me to lie with you, to plant my seed in you, so that you won't lose your father's land?"

His bold words ripped through her. But there was something lacking in the picture he drew. She wanted more. She wanted his heart as well as his body, and it was clear he was not offering it. Painfully, she withdrew her hand from his.

"I—if you do not want to . . . if it would offend you to come to our marriage bed, then there is nothing more to be said," she finished stiffly, turning her head from him.

"Hell, Katherine!" he exclaimed, drawing her eyes back to his face. "Any man would want to lie with you. I have had an impossible time trying to keep my hands from you. But you must know how difficult it would be should anything happen."

Katherine swallowed, her throat constricted with pain, and reached up to trace his cheek down to the lips that had teased and taught her the past several weeks. She whispered, "You are my husband, Daniel. I want to be your wife."

Katherine did not understand the several different expressions that crossed Daniel's face, but when his hand came up to cover hers and hold it against his cheek, she did not pull back. He turned his lips in to her hand and she thrilled to his touch.

"You are sure, Katherine?"

"Yes, Daniel. I am sure." She met his eyes bravely and waited for him to show her the way. When he said nothing, she added, "I promise I will try to please you."

With a wry grin, he said, "I doubt you will have to try very hard, my dear. You seem to have a natural talent for pleasing me. But do you know . . . that is, did your mother explain to you what marriage entails?"

"No," she said, her eyes trained on him as she shook her head. At his look of dismay, she asked, "Does it matter? Could you not tell me?"

"Would you not prefer to wait until Mrs. Burford could explain everything to you? That would give you a chance to recuperate."

Katherine stared at him in confusion. "I do not understand. What is it that must be explained?"

Daniel, a harassed look on his face, said, "I think it would be better if we waited until you talked to Mrs. Burford."

Katherine could only believe her husband had no desire for her. She had all but pleaded with him to initiate her into the secrets of marriage, yet he still refused. Embarrassed, she looked away. "I'm sorry. I thought you would want—"

"I do! It is not that I do not find you attractive, Katherine. Every time I look at you, I think about making love to you."

"Well, couldn't we try?" she asked, her hand slipping from his and moving through his black silken hair. With great daring, she leaned forward and put her lips on his, waiting for the magic she had experienced before.

His lips moved to hers, and as Katherine pressed against him, she felt his arms come around her. Their kiss deepened and she was lost in the magical sensations she had come to enjoy. It was a surprise when he held her away from him.

"Katherine," he said, taking a deep breath. "I'm not sure we should continue."

"Why not?"

With another groan, he bowed his head to her shoulder. "Because there is much more to being married, and if you don't like it, I cannot promise to stop."

Katherine whispered into his ear, "I trust you, Daniel. I know you will care for me." She loved the warmth of his body against hers.

"But you don't understand," he said impatiently, raising his head to glare at her.

"I am trying to understand, but you will not teach me!" Katherine protested, irritated that her husband refused to cooperate. "How am I to understand if you will not tell me?"

"All right," he said, "I will tell you. Married people share a bed and . . . and they lie with each other naked."

Katherine stared at him. "Are you sure?"

"Quite sure," Daniel said dryly.

With her eyes lowered to her task, Katherine reached up and began unbuttoning the high neck of her dressing gown.

Chapter Twelve

When Katherine awakened the next morning, her first thought was for the man who had shared her bed throughout the night. But he was not still in her bed. The only sign of his presence was the dent in the goose-down pillow beside her own.

But Katherine's body carried more indelible memories of her husband. Daniel had been right. There was much more to marriage than kissing. Her body ached from her husband's night-long instruction, but it was a pleasant ache, coupled with the memory of the sensations her husband had aroused.

Daniel might have been reluctant to commence their married life. In fact, Katherine was embarrassed when she thought of her boldness. But once he had begun, Daniel had demonstrated no lack of enthusiasm. And the love Katherine felt for her husband had only increased with his gentle teaching.

Katherine pushed back the covers and sat up, searching for the nightgown Daniel had helped her remove the night before. Spying it on the floor beside the bed, she leaned down and picked it up, drawing it on her body before ringing for Lucy. Her eyes were drawn to her window, and she realized the day must be well under way with the sunlight as bright as it was.

"Good morning, Lucy," Katherine greeted her maid. "What time is it?"

"It's afternoon, already, my lady, but the Master said not to awaken you," the maid explained, her eyes flying surreptitiously to the pillow beside her mistress.

Katherine's cheeks flushed, but she said nothing. A sip of hot tea from the tray Lucy brought her restored her equanimity. "Where is my husband?"

"Downstairs, my lady. He hasn't gone out of the house," she assured her mistress.

Katherine nodded. The entire household was aware of the attempt on Daniel's life by now. She knew they would be diligent in the protection of their master.

"Help me dress, Lucy. I am anxious to begin my day."

Katherine wanted to see Daniel, to feel the comfort of his presence. But she was also fearful of facing her husband. What if he had a disgust of her after last night? What if he now realized he had lost his true love by his marriage to her?

Her heart ached at the thought. She wanted her husband's love. Could she win it in time, even though he yearned for another? She didn't know the answer to that question, but she determined she would find out. She had never been one to hide from a challenge, and she would not start now.

"Good day, Katherine. How are you feeling?" Daniel asked when she finally faced him.

Katherine was disgusted that her cheeks grew pink, but she kept her chin up. "I am fine, Daniel. How have you spent your day?"

"Working on the accounts. Nothing dangerous, I can

assure you," he said with a touch of asperity. "Your servants are keeping me under close surveillance."

"*Our* servants, Daniel," Katherine corrected him, but she was unsettled by his manner. "It is only right that they have a concern for your safety."

With a sigh, Daniel sank down on the sofa. "I would take a cup of tea, if there is any left," he said, gesturing to the tea tray in front of his wife. She hurriedly served him, aware of his eyes on her the entire time.

"Thank you," Daniel murmured. An awkward silence continued for some time until Katherine asked a question about the estate. An innocuous conversation followed that did not satisfy Katherine, but at least it filled the silence.

Katherine retired to her bedroom after dinner, despair in her heart. There had been no laughter, no teasing, as they had eaten. Not once had Daniel called her his Kate. Instead, her husband had discussed his plans for the fall planting until she thought she would scream if he so much as mentioned oats again.

She must have killed even the liking her husband had for her by her behavior the night before. Tucked up in her bed, Katherine buried her face in her pillow, hoping to hide her tears from her maid. She was relieved to hear the door close behind Lucy. Turning on her back, she stared blindly into the dark.

The click of her door latch startled Katherine, and she raised up in bed. "Who's there?"

"It's me, Daniel."

Katherine's heart lurched in anticipation. "Wh-what is it, Daniel?"

He moved over to stand beside her bed, a tall shadow in the darkened room. In the same stiff voice with which he had addressed her all evening, he said, "If you want to be with child, we must continue our . . . being married, until conception is assured."

Katherine sucked in her breath. Swallowing the lump in her throat, she said, "All right."

She scooted over, waiting as he removed his robe and slid into the bed. When he reached for her, she moved eagerly into his arms. No words were spoken, but, at least for the night, Katherine was content.

As she was falling asleep, Katherine wondered if there was a way to prevent conception so that her husband would continue to share her bed.

The next several days followed the same pattern. Daniel spent his nights in Katherine's bed and his days at the desk where he worked in the Estate Room. He never mentioned the change in their relationship. He was more distant than before he had shared her bed, but in the dark, when he took her in his arms, Katherine could pretend that he loved her.

In contrast to the nights, the days were more difficult. In addition to the stiffness that existed between them, there was the threat to Daniel's life keeping him penned up in the house. It was evident to Katherine, even though she had not known her husband long, that he was chaffing under such restricted movement.

She herself longed for a gallop on Vixen, with the breeze blowing in her hair. And yet, with the danger to her husband, Katherine restricted herself as well. She could not bear the thought of anything happening to destroy her marriage.

Jesse had led his men around the estate, but Katherine knew that was no proof that the stranger was not lurking nearby, ever ready to rob her of her husband. And she feared Daniel would not be content for long with someone else fighting his battles for him.

But each morning, when he left her bed, she prayed that he might wait one more day. When on the fourth morning she asked what he would do that day and he did not respond, she knew he would wait no longer.

"Daniel? Please do not . . . be foolish. I could not bear it if anything happened to you."

"Listen to me, Kate," he said as he moved back to stand beside the bed. "I cannot hide behind these four walls forever. I must discover who is trying to kill me."

She understood his frustration, but could not accept the possibility of Daniel exposing himself to danger.

"I have left a letter with Jacob in case something should happen to me. You will be well provided for, even if the estate is lost."

"I do not care about the estate!" Katherine cried. "I don't want anything to happen to you, Daniel!"

He leaned down and kissed her long and hard, and then put her from him. "Katherine, I can cower no longer. I will do my best to remain by your side for more years than you can count. But . . ."

"I know," she said with a sigh. "What are you going to do?"

"I am only going out with Jesse and some of the lads today. There are several places they have yet to visit, and I must have some exercise. I will be fairly safe in their company."

"I pray you will, Daniel," Katherine whispered, and stared as he left the room. "Dear God, please let him come back safely."

With Daniel no longer in the house, Katherine was not content to fill her time with an inventory of the linens, or the planning of the weekly menus. The urge to ride grew stronger, and she decided a visit to Betsy would be in order. She had not seen her friend since the day they rode into the village.

Remembering Daniel's anger the last time, she informed Greyson of her intent and changed into her riding habit. Then, at the stables, she enlisted two grooms to ride with her, though in truth she felt sure there was no danger for herself.

The Drakes' estate was only a half-hour ride from White Oaks, and Katherine rode beneath the trees on the cool afternoon with enjoyment. Her arrival met with great happiness, Betsy hugging her in delight.

"I was going to write you a note this afternoon and ask if I might call on you. Are you feeling much more the thing?" she asked even as she looked carefully at her friend.

Katherine smiled. "I am feeling fine, Betsy."

"Yes, I can see you are." With a wide smile, Betsy added, "I am also."

Katherine looked at Betsy closely. "You have something important to tell me. What is it?"

Blushing, Betsy said, "Jack came this morning to talk to my father. He has asked for my hand in marriage."

With a scream of delight, Katherine hugged her friend again. "Oh, Betsy, I am so happy for you. The two of you make a delightful couple."

"Thank you," Betsy said, her delight shining in her face. "I had dreamed of it for so long. He did not tell me . . . that is, we had grown closer since Daniel's arrival, what with the dancing lessons and our visits, but . . . I was not sure . . . he surprised me!"

"You mean he finally came to his senses. You will be a wonderful wife to him. And we will be close neighbors, and raise our children together. Oh, Betsy, nothing could make me happier."

Something in her manner caused Betsy to ask, "Are you happy with your marriage?"

"Yes, of course I am," Katherine said, and both young women ignored the hesitancy in her voice. Katherine paused as her eyes darkened. "If only this stranger, whoever he is, would be captured."

Betsy reached out to squeeze her friend's hands. "I am sure someone will see him. Jack said he had sent several of his men out each day to ride the roads and neighborhood, looking for some sign of the man. After he and his father rode about the neighborhood telling everyone of the danger, others agreed that he must be found."

"Yes. But today Daniel has ridden out to look."

"Oh, no. That is dangerous, is it not?"

"Yes, but Daniel is not one to hide behind others," Katherine said with pride. "He insists on looking himself."

"He is not alone?"

"No, some of our men are accompanying him." Katherine sighed. "But I will be relieved when he returns home."

"I am surprised he gave you permission to ride over here."

Katherine did not meet her friend's inquiring look. "Well, he did not exactly give me permission. He had already left when I decided to come. But I brought along two grooms."

"I hope he does not become angry with you again." Betsy shuddered as she remembered their reception when they returned from the village.

"He will not." Katherine turned the conversation back to her friend's engagement and wedding, taking her mind off her worrisome thoughts. Betsy was quite willing to discuss topics so close to her heart, and most of the afternoon was whiled away with talk of weddings.

Katherine jumped when the hall clock struck four. "Oh, my, I did not realize it was so late. I must hurry home. Daniel will be returning soon."

With just the thought, she longed to see her husband so intensely she scarcely remembered saying good-bye to her friend. The two grooms brought her horse around, and she waved good-bye as she set her mount at a fast pace.

As she rode along, she thought about Betsy's good news and the enjoyment she would have living close to her best friend.

Their children would be able to play with each other, and . . . It suddenly occurred to Katherine that she might already be carrying Daniel's child. That thought sent all others scurrying from her mind.

"Is anything wrong, my lady?" Willie, one of the grooms, asked.

"What?" Katherine responded, dragged back to reality.

"Well, you slowed down, like something might be wrong."

"Oh, no, sorry, Willie. I was just not paying attention. Everything is fine." She urged her horse to a trot.

They were almost halfway home when the path curved to the left near a big tree. Katherine was thinking of her return, eager to see Daniel, when a large bay horse suddenly appeared before them. Sitting on the horse was a rough-looking dark-haired man, a pistol in each hand.

"Whoa, there, my friends," the man growled.

Katherine knew at once that she had found the Canadian. If nothing else, the accent would have given him away.

"What do you want?" she demanded, determined not to show her fear.

"Ah, the little woman is brave, is she not? What I want is you, *ma petite*."

"Here now," Willie said, pushing his mount forward. "You can't be bothering Lady St. Cloud."

Without a word of warning, the man fired one of the two pistols in his hands, and Willie fell to the ground without a sound.

"No!" Katherine screamed and started to dismount.

"Stay where you are!" the man ordered, his second pistol pointed at her heart.

Katherine gulped for air and then said, "He needs help. Please let me help him."

"He is of no importance." Putting the gun that he had fired in his belt, the man reached behind him and drew forth a piece of rope. He tossed it to the other stablehand riding with Katherine. "Tie your lady's hands behind her back. And be quick about it."

"Sorry, my lady," the young man mumbled as he did as he was told.

Katherine, breathing rapidly to hold back her sobs, whispered, "It does not matter, Peter. Try to help Willie if he . . . leaves you here."

When her hands were tied, the foreigner ordered Peter off his horse. Riding closer, he took Katherine's reins in his free hand. "Now," he ordered Peter, "send your horse away."

Peter swatted his horse with a yell and sent him galloping off down the path, followed closely by Willie's horse.

"Well done, my friend," he said in a hateful tones. "Now, you may walk back to the estate. And inform Lord St. Cloud that if he desires to see his wife ever again, he must come for her himself. I will deal with no one else."

"No, Peter, do not tell him! He must not—"

The pistol felt cold against her ear, halting Katherine's protest. "A wise decision, *ma petite*." He turned back to Peter. "Tell him what I said." Without waiting for the servant's agreement to his order, he jerked the reins of Katherine's horse and rode off into the forest.

Peter was a big lad, but only fifteen years old. However, he did not panic. He first determined that Willie was still breathing. Taking off his shirt, he ripped it apart to bind his friend's wound. Since Willie was still unconscious, Peter dragged him a few feet to where he would be in the shade but still visible should anyone come along to help him. Then with a final look at his friend, Peter loped down the path toward White Oaks.

The ride had released some of Daniel's tension at being cooped up in the house for several days, but it had produced no new leads about the stranger who threatened his life. When they rode back into the stables, he thanked the men who had accompanied him, then walked up to the house. He was eager to see Katherine. She was fast becoming an obsession to him.

When he reached the main hall, Greyson greeted him with signs of relief.

"Where is your mistress?"

"She had not yet returned, my lord. But may I say we are pleased you have arrived safe and sound?" Greyson said with a smile.

"Not returned? Where has she gone?" Daniel demanded, an angry frown on his face.

"Why, she rode over to the Drakes, sir. She took two of the lads from the stable with her. I watched them ride off to be sure."

"What time is it now?"

"Almost half past four. She should be home any time now."

"All right. I'm going to change. Let me know as soon as she is sighted," Daniel asked, telling himself not to become overset. After all, the man had not tried to harm Katherine, only himself. And she had two men with her for protection. He could not wrap his wife in cotton wool, or keep her in the house. She had become as restless as he at not being able to ride.

He went upstairs and washed and changed with Jacob's assistance, one ear constantly cocked for news of Katherine. He came back downstairs to find Greyson at his post. "No word of Lady St. Cloud yet?"

"No sir. It is almost five. I thought she would have returned by now."

Daniel moved toward the front door and looked out the windows beside it. "I would have thought so." Even as he stared, a movement alerted him. "Greyson, someone is running down the path."

The butler hurried to stand beside his master. "It looks like . . . like Peter. He accompanied Lady St. Cloud!"

Daniel had wrenched open the door, and was halfway to the man before Greyson had finished speaking. The butler grabbed a passing maid. "Send to the stables. Something has happened to Miss Katherine. The men are to saddle the horses and get ready." Then he hurried after his master.

Chapter Thirteen

Katherine hung on as best she could with her hands tied. Her captor spared no thought for her comfort as he plowed through the underlying brush. He also made no attempt to conceal their direction.

Though she considered different avenues of escape, none recommended itself to her. But she was sure she was the bait to trap Daniel. She could not wait to be rescued. She needed to help herself. Therefore, when the burly man ahead of her slowed the pace to a fast walk because of the undergrowth, Katherine kicked her feet free from the stirrups and lifted her right leg from the hook of her sidesaddle.

With as little commotion as possible, she slid from the saddle, landing with a thud. The man might not have noticed her dismount had it not been for Vixen's squeal of protest and sidling away from her. Before Katherine could rise and run, he was off his horse and beside her.

"Listen, my lovely! Any more such behavior and I'll tie you like a sack hanging over your saddle. Do you understand?"

"Y-yes," she whispered, drawing back from her

captor, his foul breath and dirty hands sending shivers of distaste over her.

He yanked her upright and shoved her roughly back into her saddle. Taking the rope that bound her hands, he tied the end of it to her saddle. "Now, should you fall, you'll be dragged along like a useless dog."

Katherine made no response, staring straight ahead. She ached all over and despair was growing. This villain's casual shooting of Willie and his attempts to kill Daniel showed he had no respect for human life. She knew he would never spare her. And if Daniel was to die, she did not think she wanted to be spared.

"*Vraiment*, I never expected an Englishwoman to have such spirit, little one. I will have to give you that . . . and a certain beauty," the bearded man said, resting his hand on her thigh.

Katherine detested his touch, but to protest would only invite more, she felt sure. Ignoring his taunt, she waited for him to continue their journey.

After a moment, he remounted and continued to wherever he was taking her. Katherine tried to determine their destination, but he seemed to be going in circles.

Finally, they broke into a clearing. Katherine could hear a stream gurgling along somewhere near, and there was a ramshackle hut built against the face of a cliff, but it was not the hut located on their property. The man pulled their horses to a halt and dismounted. Turning back to Katherine, he untied the rope from the saddle and then yanked her off, catching her unawares. Since she had not freed her feet from the stirrups, she fell hard on her shoulder and face.

"Sorry, my lady," he said, laughing, as he mocked her with an elegant bow. Then, in a hard voice, he ordered, "Into the hut."

Katherine struggled to her feet. She could feel blood

oozing from a scrape on her cheek, and her shoulder ached, but she made no protest. With her chin high, she obeyed his orders.

As soon as she entered, he shoved her into a wooden chair. Untying her hands, he then wrenched them behind her back and retied them to the chair. The tightness of the knot was a constant pain. He then tied her feet together.

"There now, my fine lady. See how comfortable I have made you?" He turned to leave. "Do not worry. I shall return as soon as I have hidden my horse. I want to make a fast escape as soon as I have dealt with your husband . . . and you."

Katherine shuddered as he disappeared. His evil eyes conveyed the surety of his words. She thought of Daniel, and the little time they had had together. She wished now she had told him how much she loved him. He had become the center of her world. Whatever horrible death this man intended to deal her, she had at least had those few days with Daniel.

If only she could find a way to warn her husband. He might not be a St. Cloud, but he deserved to live. And she knew he would take care of their people and manage the estate well. God must have been watching over her when she chose Daniel to play his role. She could not have a better person . . . to be her cousin or her husband.

"Oh, Daniel," she murmured, "please take care!"

"What happened?" Daniel demanded of Peter as he reached him.

Peter, having run the entire way, was completely out of breath. "A m-man . . . he took . . . m-my lady. Willie . . ."

"When? Where did he take them?"

"He—he didn't take . . . Willie . . . he shot him."

"Did he hurt Lady St. Cloud?" Daniel demanded, fear in his voice.

"N-no! No, sir. He made me . . . tie her hands and he took her a-away. Said you were to come . . . if you wanted to s-see her again. An' Willie's hurt bad."

Daniel whirled to race for the stables as Greyson reached them. The butler explained he had already alerted the stables. Daniel turned back to Peter. "Can you show me where he left the path?"

"Yes, my lord."

"Greyson, we'll need the doctor. Willie's been shot. Send for him, and I'll order a wagon brought around."

Daniel's mind was sifting through what little information Peter had given him as he raced toward the stables. He was met halfway by several grooms leading two other horses. He took the two horses and sent one of the men back to ask for a wagon and more men.

When he returned to the front of the house, he discovered Peter and Greyson had been joined by Squire Burford and his wife and son. They were in their carriage and elegantly dressed in evening clothes.

Jack had descended from the carriage. As Daniel rode up, he moved toward him. "If you will lend me a mount, I will accompany you."

"Thank you. Peter, take this horse and ride back to the stables and get another for Mr. Burford. And go to the gun room and bring us some arms."

"What do you know?" Jack asked.

"Not much. But I suspect he is setting a trap for me. He told Peter if I wanted—wanted to see Katherine alive, I must be the one to come to her rescue."

Jack gripped Daniel's shoulder. "Perhaps you should

consider allowing me to lead your men. Katherine would never forgive me if anything happened to you."

"No! I must rescue Katherine, whether there is a trap or not. I will just have to outwit this man, whoever he is. He has already shot one of the men riding with Katherine. We must not waste time."

"Shouldn't you wait for more men to ride with you?" Squire Burford asked anxiously.

"We already outnumber him. No, more men will not help. He has some kind of plan that ensures his safety no matter how many men we have," Daniel said intensely. "We must outthink him."

Squire Burford and his wife watched as the men arrived with more horses and guns. As they prepared to depart, the squire said, "I'll go on to the Drakes' and round up more men, just in case. We'll follow as soon as possible."

Daniel only nodded. He would take time later to express his gratitude for his neighbor's assistance. Now, his mind dwelt only on his wife.

After a few moments, Katherine calmed down, drawing deep breaths, and surveyed her surroundings. The hut, from outside, was old and almost falling down. But inside, someone had done a lot of work. The walls were well braced, and the only window was in the front, alongside the door. A heavy piece of timber had been placed in the window brackets, making it impossible to break in from the outside.

There was a companion piece of timber resting against the wall to be used on the door. The man must feel confident that his enemy would not be arriving soon. But Katherine was puzzled. He might be able to withstand an army inside, but how would he escape? Even if he tried to use the two of them as shields, it would be very dangerous.

And if he was taking all this time to hide his horse, it must not be close to the hut. And if that was true, how would he escape as quickly as he had said? She frowned in thought.

Her eyes surveyed the walls, looking for a different way out, but she could find nothing. Suddenly she thought about a cavern beneath the floor. Perhaps there was a trap door, leading to an exit unknown to her. She studied the floor planking, but she could find nothing that would give indication of a secret door.

Frustrated, she twisted against her bonds. If she could outthink this villain, perhaps she could help Daniel. If they were to have any chance at all, he would need every advantage.

"Dear God," she prayed, raising her eyes in desperation, and saw a strange sight. There, over in the corner, extending down from the ceiling, hung a rope. She might have thought it a crude bellpull, but there were no servants to respond in a one-room hut. It was growing dim as the day dwindled, and she strained her eyes as she looked carefully, gradually distinguishing traces of light coming through the ceiling, as if the roof above that section was more lightly laid.

Why would there be a rope hanging down unless it was to allow the man to climb to the roof? But what purpose would that serve? He would be more exposed there than he would be in the cabin. Katherine tried to visualize the roof to search for an escape route. Her mind flashed a picture of the hut as they arrived. It was backed to a wall of rock, very steep but not too high. Suddenly, Katherine understood his plan.

The man intended to climb the rope to the top of the cliff. She was sure he must have hidden his horse up there. In the dark, it would be hard to shoot him, and he would have reached the top, mounted, and ridden off before the others had a chance to ride to the nearest path up the hill.

Satisfied that she had figured out his plan, Katherine then had to decide how that information would help Daniel. If only she could warn him before he entered the cabin. But that was an impossible thought. The man would have returned long before he expected Daniel to arrive. And she knew he would not be gentle, should she try to signal her husband.

Even that would not stop her if she could think of something that would tell Daniel of his escape route. She didn't think she would have time to say much. Her mind in turmoil, she waited for the return of her captor.

The men rode swiftly back up the path, leaving the wagon in the distance. Peter, riding at the front next to his master, strained his eyes to see ahead. He was worried about Willie, and he was frightened for his mistress.

Daniel's lips were pressed tightly together. Every minute seemed like an hour to him. Over and over in his heart, he said Katherine's name, a silent prayer for her safety.

"There's Willie," Peter called, turning his horse to the side of the road where he had left his friend. Daniel wanted to ride on and leave Willie to those who were following, but he forced himself to be patient. He dismounted and followed Peter to the injured man's side.

"Is he alive?"

"I don't know, my lord," Peter said, his voice shaking.

The wound was in the chest and blood covered Willie's body. Daniel knelt down and felt for a pulse. He was relieved to find a faint one. "He's alive, Peter. Show me where the man left the path and then you stay here with Willie. You've done a good job."

"I'll show you, Master, but I'm going on with you. Willie would want me to. And I wouldn't mind a chance at that villain to make up for what he did to Willie." Sudden guilt appeared on Peter's face as he added, "And my lady! I just forgot for a minute, my lord."

"It's all right, Peter. Did you get a gun?"

"Yes, sir."

"Harry," Daniel called to one of the older men. "You stay with Willie and help get him home. The rest of you come with us."

The stranger returned a few minutes later. Katherine sat still, watching his every move. "Well, well, *ma petite,* did you think I had forgotten about you?"

She did not answer, only staring at him with large, blue eyes.

"I must say, Daniel has good taste in his women."

Ignoring the compliment, Katherine realized something important. "You know my husband?"

There was a hearty laugh, and the dark man said, "*Oui,* I know your husband. We once spent the winter trapping together."

"Then . . . then why are you trying to kill him?"

"I am not trying, little one. I will kill him." His blunt answer drove what little color there was from her cheeks. "I am sorry to distress such a pretty one as you."

He strolled over to capture her chin in his cruel hand and tilt her face up to him. "Yes, you are a pretty thing." Without warning, he swooped down and covered her lips with his. Katherine twisted and turned to get away from him, but he held her firmly in place. When he lifted his head, she shot him a fiery look and turned sideways and spat.

His anger was evident, but he brought it under control. "You think you are too good for me? You will pay for your behavior, woman. I will let you pleasure my body before you die." He enjoyed Katherine's gasp. "But I will wait until I have your husband for an audience. Daniel will hate that," he said with enjoyment. "Then I'll kill you both, slowly."

Katherine said nothing, struggling to hide her fears from the hateful man. She would not give him the pleasure of seeing her cry . . . or beg. When she was under control, she asked the question that had bothered her from the very beginning.

"Why do you want to kill my husband? What has he done?"

"Ah. You mean other than being unbearably lucky?"

"What do you mean?" Katherine demanded.

"Daniel's father died when he was two. His mother remarried. Most stepfathers are hateful, mean," the man said, memory marking his face, "but Daniel? He got a kind stepfather. And a rich one. Robert Hawthorne is one of the richest fur traders and shippers in the New World. Daniel is handsome and rich, and all the women want him. Then he inherited this property and title here in England. Every woman he knew wanted him to marry her and bring her back to England to lord it over everyone."

Katherine hoped she concealed how surprised she was to discover that Daniel was her real cousin, who had come to claim his inheritance. "So you have tried to kill him because you are jealous?"

"*Non, petite imbécile*. I am going to kill him so that *I* will be lucky."

"I do not understand."

"When someone receives proof of Daniel's death, I will be given five thousand pounds." The man smacked his lips in anticipation.

Katherine stared at him in horror. "You would kill for money?" she gasped.

"Of course. I kill the furry animals for money. Why not Daniel?" he asked with a hearty chuckle that raised the hair on the back of Katherine's neck.

Now she knew she must try to warn Daniel of the man's escape route. She must ensure that he be caught, if nothing else. She turned her head away. She wanted no more conversation. It was important that she hear Daniel's arrival.

The man busied himself building a fire. When the kindling caught, he fanned it to a brightly burning flame, adding a little light to the gloom of the hut. Then he turned to survey Katherine. She shivered but said nothing.

"Hmmm. I think I shall have need of your jacket."

"Why would you want my jacket?" Katherine demanded.

"As a flag for your loving husband, *ma petite*." He moved behind her to untie the tight bonds. As soon as her hands were free, he pulled a large knife and held it to her throat. "Now, remove your jacket."

Katherine shrugged out of the modish blue riding jacket with as little movement as possible, since every move pressed her neck into the knife's blade. A thin rivulet of blood ran down her neck into her blouse.

The man took her jacket, retied her hands, and walked to the front door. Opening it, he affixed the jacket to the latch and then pulled the door to, lowering the timber in place. He turned back to look at his prisoner. "You have much to offer a man," he said as he stared at her bosom outlined in her fine white blouse. "Perhaps I will sample a little of your bounty before your husband's arrival."

Katherine almost stopped breathing as he took a step toward her. She could not bear the thought of the man touching her. But a sound halted him. With a regretful look at his quarry, he ran over to the window, where a small peephole had been cut.

Peter found the break in the underbrush, showing the man's path. Daniel and Jack exchanged looks and followed in the boy's wake. There was no difficulty in following the trail. As Daniel had suspected, the man wanted to be found.

Jack pushed his horse up beside Daniel. "I agree this is a baited trap. Don't you think you should hang back and let me deal with this?"

"No, Jack. Thank you for your offer, but I am the cause of all the difficulties. I must be the one to take care of it."

"Have you figured out what to do?"

"No. That will be impossible until I see where he is holding her. But I hope we reach it soon. The sun is almost gone."

It was only a quarter of an hour later that the group of men reached the clearing, with the hut clearly visible to everyone. Daniel halted his group while they still had the trees for cover.

There was smoke coming up the crude chimney, but even more telling was the blue riding jacket with the frogging on it hanging on the door. Daniel recognized it as Katherine's. "He's got her in there," he muttered in a deadly voice that sent shivers down Jack's spine.

"What do we do now?" Jack asked in a low voice.

"I want the men to spread out about the clearing.

Whatever happens, I don't want him to escape. Do you understand?" Daniel demanded grimly.

"He will not," Jack assured him. "But what are you going to do?"

"I am going to go talk to him. That is what he wants. That's why he hung Katherine's jacket on the latch."

"But Daniel, he could shoot you down before you ever reach the door."

"I know, Jack," Daniel said as he continued to study the hut. "But I don't think that's what he wants to do." He started to urge his horse forward, but then he stopped. "I don't understand."

"What?" Jack asked.

"How will he escape?"

"I told you I would ensure he will not."

"No, Jack, you don't understand. The man, whoever he is, has planned this entire meeting. If it were you, would you forget to plan an escape?" Daniel asked.

"No, of course not. You are right, Daniel. I should have thought of that."

"Perhaps I have had more experience at hunting than you, Jack," Daniel said dryly.

"But every fox has a second way out of its hole. I should have remembered that."

Daniel sighed. "Well, that is beside the point. The real question is what is his plan?"

The two men conferred for several minutes, but in the end, Daniel could wait no more. He headed for the hut.

"Aha!" the Canadian exclaimed, his eye to the peephole.

"What is it?" Katherine called, fear tightening in her throat.

"Your husband has arrived. He and a group of others are hovering in the woods." He watched silently, saying nothing else, and Katherine debated whether to call her warning now. But the trees were not close to the hut, and she must be sure Daniel would hear her. She would only have one chance.

The man gave a delighted chuckle.

"What is happening?" Katherine demanded huskily.

"Your husband is dispersing his troops. He thinks he can prevent my escape."

Katherine forced herself not to look at the rope in the corner. Once the man knew she had figured out his plan, she feared he would gag her.

"Now what is he doing?" he muttered, as he continued to stare out the opening.

Katherine waited in tense silence.

"Ah, now he is coming. Alone. I knew Daniel would understand," the man said gleefully.

"What are you going to do?"

"I am going to enjoy myself, woman. After I ravish you, I shall kill both of you. Won't that be pleasant?" he demanded, a frightening grimace on his face.

Katherine bit her lip, breathing deeply, determined not to show her fear.

"Hello?" Daniel's voice drew the man's attention.

"Hello, Daniel."

"Who is that?"

"It is Jean-Paul, *mon ami.*"

Daniel did not respond at once, and Katherine waited, holding her breath. "Jean-Paul? Do you have my wife in there with you?"

"But of course I do, Daniel."

"What do you want, Jean-Paul?"

"I want you," the Canadian called out gaily.

"As soon as you release my wife, I will give you what you want," Daniel promised.

"Ah, but you do not know all my wants, my friend. I

want you to get off your horse, put down your arms, and enter the cabin. Then we will talk."

Katherine watched the man, her only guide to what was happening. When he relaxed, she knew Daniel was following his directions. Now was the time.

"The roof, Dan—"

Chapter Fourteen

At the sound of Katherine's voice, Daniel lunged forward, but even as he did so, he puzzled over her words. He heard a thud as her voice stopped, and he knew she had paid dearly for her warning. But why those words?

He halted and looked at the hut. The light was dim and fading fast. He could see nothing about the roof to make Katherine . . . the sound of a horse neighing caught his attention. It did not come from behind him but in front. Unless Jean-Paul had his horse in the hut, that was impossible. The sound was repeated, and this time Daniel's sharp ears traced the sound to the cliff above the hut.

Searching the wall of the cliff, he found what he looked for. Turning around, he motioned quickly to Jack, pointing to the top of the cliff. He hoped his friend realized what he was saying, because he had no more time.

"Daniel?"

"Yes, Jean-Paul?"

"You'd better get in here. Your little wife needs you."

Hurrying forward, Daniel slid through the opening of the door. He knew without looking Jean-Paul would be behind the door with his pistol at the ready. But he was more interested in Katherine.

Jean-Paul had struck her and the force of his blow had knocked her chair on its side, causing her to strike her head. She'd lost consciousness on impact.

"Katherine? Katherine?" Daniel called to her, bringing her awake.

"Daniel?" she whispered.

"Yes, sweetheart. I'm here."

"I'm very glad you are," Jean-Paul drawled. *"Tu me plais beaucoup, mon ami."*

Daniel examined his wife and turned, enraged, to the other man. "You are inhuman to do this to her!"

"Inhuman? No, *mon ami,* I am very human. I intend to demonstrate that to you soon." The cruelty in the man's voice chilled Daniel's anger. He must not let his emotions interfere with his thinking.

"Lift up your wife's chair, Daniel. We do not want her to lie on the floor, do we?"

Daniel eyed the man standing over him. He did not want to turn his back on him, so he moved around the chair and lifted Katherine up from the other side.

"Ah, you were always the smart one, Daniel." He stared at the pair. "Now it appears I will have to shoot you first, since you do not want to be knocked out." He smirked. "Do not worry. You will not die from it . . . yet."

Katherine could not stop shaking. Were it not for the ropes, she would have fallen to the floor again. Tears spurted from her eyes in spite of her efforts to show no fear.

Daniel did not look at his wife. It would only destroy his concentration. Whatever Jean-Paul had in mind,

Katherine was already frightened. He moved in front of Katherine and gauged the distance between him and his attacker carefully. There was no time to wait.

Jean-Paul had the gun aimed at his legs and Daniel leaped in midair, throwing his body at his adversary. Jean-Paul, concentrating on the torture he intended to inflict, was caught unawares. The gun discharged as Daniel hit him, and the two rolled in the floor. Katherine screamed without even realizing it. Fear clutched her heart as she watched the two men struggle.

The sound of horses running changed her screams to cries for help, But Jean-Paul had placed the timber through the bars, making it impossible for anyone to enter. Pounding on the door, someone called through it.

"Jack? Jack, please help!" Katherine called.

"We can't get in, Katherine. Can you unbolt the door?"

"No. I'm tied up. Please, Jack. I'm afraid."

She could hear movement, but there was no visible progress. She watched, horror-stricken, as the two men rolled about the floor, their fists flailing. Suddenly her earlier warning to Daniel flashed in her mind. "The roof! Jack, there is a hole in the roof!"

"Right," was the muffled response.

Katherine tried to scoot her chair closer, hoping to kick the villain as the two fought, but they moved too fast for her awkward progress. "Please, God, please let them come. Please don't let Daniel be hurt," she prayed in whispers, as her eyes followed the fight.

Suddenly Jean-Paul broke free of Daniel and found the knife he had used against Katherine earlier. Now the tempo of the fight changed. The two men circled the room, one taking dangerous swipes and the other avoiding him with balletic grace. Each time Katherine gasped, sure Daniel would fall to the floor.

Then, several things happened at once. There was movement on the roof and a man's feet appeared as he came down the rope. That distracted Jean-Paul enough to allow Daniel to close in on him. The two fell to the floor as Jack's head appeared in the room. Katherine never even looked at him, her eyes fastened on the two men grappling on the floor. There was a gasp and blood spurted into the air. Katherine, unable to determine who had been stabbed, fainted.

Katherine came to a second time resting on her husband's shoulder while someone was untying her hands. "Daniel? You are all right?" she gasped.

"Yes, my love. You are safe now. Just relax. Jack will have your hands untied in a moment."

"That—that man?"

"He has been disposed of," Daniel said in a hard voice.

Katherine buried her face into his neck. She didn't want to know anymore. At least not at the moment.

As soon as Jack had untied her hands, he unlocked the door of the cabin to reassure the others.

Daniel untied her feet and then scooped her up into his arms, cuddling her close to him. Katherine had no complaints. She had thought to never feel those arms around her again. It was such a heavenly place to be, she thought dreamily.

"I think she has passed out again," Daniel said quietly to Jack. "If you will hold her until I am on my horse, I will carry her home."

"It is almost an hour away, Daniel. Will you not be tired?"

"I will never tire of holding her, Jack. I almost lost her this evening," Daniel reminded him, and Jack said nothing else.

Katherine felt herself being moved about, but she gave up the effort to remain conscious. Her dreamy state was so much more comfortable . . . and it seemed she had been uncomfortable for a long time.

When next Katherine returned to consciousness, she was being taken from that warm, comfortable haven of Daniel's arms and handed to others. She struggled to move as she whispered, "Daniel?"

He swung down from his horse and took Katherine back in his arms. "I am here, sweetheart. I'm going to carry you up to your bed so the doctor can examine you."

There seemed to be more people around, but Katherine paid them no attention. She only needed Daniel.

When she was placed in her bed, Daniel kissed her brow and whispered that he would return shortly. Katherine's eyes followed his broad back as he left her room. Then she realized there were several people around her bed. Betsy, Mrs. Drake, and Mrs. Burford were all there, as well as Lucy and Flora. In no time, they had her washed and dressed in a nightgown.

The doctor examined her with gentle hands, but the cuts she had sustained on her neck and face were painful. He bandaged her and put salve on her scraped cheek. "I do not think your concussion is severe, my lady. If you feel like rising from your bed tomorrow, you may do so, but do not ride until after I have examined you again."

"Yes, Doctor," Katherine said hoarsely, surprised to discover her throat sore.

"That will pass," he assured her. "It is from the strain of your voice during your kidnapping."

"Thank you. Betsy, why—why are all of you here?" she asked as the doctor departed.

"The Burfords were on their way to our house for a

dinner to celebrate our engagement when they discovered what had happened. Jack went with Daniel, but the squire and Mrs. Burford came to our estate. Father and the squire organized some of our men and rode after the others, but they got there only after it was all over."

"I—I'm sorry we spoiled your evening," Katherine said.

Mrs. Drake smiled warmly at Katherine. "Pshaw, child, we're just glad everything turned out all right. We can get these two young people engaged without sitting down at the dinner table."

"Or you can sit down at our dinner table and celebrate their union," Daniel said, surprising the women. He moved into the room. "Apparently Cook has been preparing food since we left to be sure she had all in readiness. Greyson is ready to serve you and your menfolk in the dining room."

"That is not necessary!" Mrs. Burford said. "You cannot want to bother feeding us right now."

"Well, in point of fact, I had not intended to join you. I want to eat here with Katherine, but Greyson will attend you." Daniel grinned at the ladies. "You will be doing us a favor if you will dine here. Someone must eat all of the prepared food, and it gives those who did not accompany us the opportunity to feel they have served their mistress too."

"Yes, of course," Mrs. Burford said, capitulating to his logic. "You are wise, my lord. We will go down at once. But may we just say how pleased we are that everything turned out all right, and that we are grateful you came into our midst."

"Thank you, ma'am," Daniel said gravely. Looking at Katherine, he murmured, "I am quite happy to be here."

Mrs. Drake smiled and also looked at Katherine, whose eyes were trained on her husband. "Yes, well, we'll go down to eat and leave the two of you to enjoy a little peace and quiet. That will be a novel experience for you, won't it?"

Daniel smiled in return and held the door for the ladies. Then he turned to the two maids. "You have both served us well, Lucy and Flora. Thank you. Why do you not go down and join in the banquet in the kitchen as soon as you have brought up our trays."

The two maids beamed at him and slipped from the room. Finally, Daniel and Katherine were alone. Daniel wasted no time taking his wife in his arms.

Katherine lay against her husband, relishing his closeness. A shudder passed through her as she thought about how close she had come to never feeling his arms around her again.

"Do not think about it, my Kate," Daniel whispered, holding her tighter.

"He was so evil!"

"I could not believe Jean-Paul could be so inhuman," Daniel muttered.

"He said he was going to kill you for money, Daniel. Someone was paying him five thousand pounds to kill you," Katherine said, her hands sliding down her husband's back.

Daniel released her to sit up and stare at her. "That's what he meant!" he exclaimed.

"What, Daniel?"

"Jean-Paul kept repeating Henry's name. I couldn't understand why, but he must have been trying to tell me that it was Henry who hired him to kill me."

Katherine reached up a finger to smooth out the frown on his forehead. "Who is Henry?"

"A cousin of sorts. He is my stepfather's nephew."

Katherine's hand slid to the back of Daniel's neck, her

fingers weaving into his hair. "Why would he want—want to harm you?"

"I am my stepfather's heir."

Katherine's hand stilled. "And why would that make him want to kill you?" she asked.

Daniel moved closer to his wife and touched the bandage on her cheek. "Does this hurt?" he asked.

"No. Daniel, explain," Katherine insisted, catching his hand.

"What?" Daniel asked, distracted. "Oh, my stepfather is wealthy," he added as his lips trailed from her bandage to her lips.

"So," Katherine said between the kisses her husband was bestowing on her, "when you received word of your inheritance, you really had no need of it?"

"Not really," Daniel said, his lips now caressing Katherine's throat.

"And that is why you came here as Daniel Hawthorne rather than Daniel St. Cloud?"

Katherine knew the second her words penetrated Daniel's mind, because his delicious nibbling ceased and he pulled back to stare at her.

"You know?"

"That man, Jean-Paul, gave you away."

Daniel looked shamefaced as he protested, "I did not intend to mislead you, love, but you were so beautiful and earnest, I could not resist."

"When I think of the worries I suffered, wondering who you were, what kind of man you were!" Katherine protested, shoving against her husband's broad chest.

He grinned as he captured her hand and held it against him. "I know."

"Oh, you monster! Enjoying my difficulties." In spite of her words, a smile was quivering on Katherine's lips.

Daniel leaned forward to kiss the corner of her lips.

"Truly, my Kate, I did intend to tell you in a few days, but then we were attacked by the highwaymen and everything changed."

"Yes," Katherine agreed, her face sobering.

"Will you forgive me, Katherine? And will you forgive me for bringing my enemies here to hurt you?"

Katherine's hand rubbed against his chest where he still held it. "You could not have known such a thing would occur."

"I would not bring harm to you, my bonny Kate."

"I know. But what are you going to do about your cousin? He could hire someone else," Katherine gasped as that horrible thought occurred to her. "Oh, Daniel, surely we will not have to go through that again?"

Daniel crushed her against him. "I promise you will not, my sweet. I'll write my stepfather and inform him of Henry's actions. Henry hasn't hidden his hate for me, but he knew my stepfather would punish him severely if he thought Henry had tried to hurt me. I suspect he saw my trip to England as a godsend, allowing him to hire Jean-Paul and maintain a pretense of innocence himself in Montreal."

He paused to press a kiss against her temple before adding, "Without evidence, he will not be able to put him in prison, but my stepfather will know how to handle Henry so that he will never be a threat to us again."

There was a discreet knock at the door before the two maids entered, each bearing a tray. Daniel waited patiently while the servants arranged their meal before departing. As the door closed behind them, he poured two glasses of wine. "I'm not sure you should drink this after your concussion, but I think a toast would be appropriate."

"I do not think it would harm me," Katherine said

with a smile. "It is hard to believe the nightmare has ended, isn't it, Daniel?"

"Our marriage will be so mundane from this day forward, my Kate, you will complain of boredom."

Katherine surveyed her husband, his large, muscular body fit and virile, his dark hair curling around his head, his blue eyes sparkling, and knew marriage to him would never be boring. "I do not think I will complain, Daniel."

He handed her a glass of wine and raised his own. "To our marriage, my love. May it be a long and happy one." Their glasses clinked as they touched before each sipped the wine. "You will be happy to know the doctor said Willie will recover, after a sufficient period of recuperation."

"I am glad," Katherine said before setting down her glass and leaning back against the pillows, staring at her husband. "Daniel, there is something I must know."

He looked up in surprise. "I will tell you anything, my Kate."

"I—I must know the identity of the woman to whom you were attracted at the picnic and the Cranes' party."

She could see her question surprised him. He set down his wine glass and folded his arms as he leaned on the table beside the bed. "That is your question?"

"Yes. I know I should not ask it. But . . . but I must know. I cannot live with you as your wife knowing you are longing for some other woman and . . . and not know who she is. I would be constantly asking myself if it was her every time we went out in society." Katherine nibbled on her bottom lip and watched her husband with anxious eyes.

"I will tell you, if you are sure you want to know," Daniel assured her, grinning.

"Well, I wish you would not look as if you are

enjoying our conversation!" Katherine protested. "I find this very difficult."

When he continued to grin at her but said nothing, Katherine asked, "Is it Lady Priscilla?" She cringed as though fearful of his response.

"Of course not, my bonny Kate. She can not hold a candle to you."

His answer pleased her, but there was still the identity of the unknown woman. "If it is not her, then who could it be?"

Daniel stared at her steadily, saying nothing.

"Daniel! You must tell me!"

"Why must I tell you?" he asked in reasonable tones. "Have I asked you to reveal your heart to me? You are my wife, Katherine. I ask nothing more of you."

"I know," Katherine whispered, tears welling up in her eyes. "I wish. . . ."

"What do you wish, my dear?" Daniel asked, concern in his voice.

Raising her chin, Katherine said, "Daniel, I must tell you something. I . . . while I was in that hut with J-Jean-Paul, I realized I should have told you before." She looked away from his piercing eyes and her fingers plucked restively at her covers.

Daniel reached out and covered her hand, his warmth a shock to her cold fingers. "What is it, Katherine?"

"I—I did not marry you to p-please my mother."

Daniel grew still but said nothing.

Katherine flashed a look at his face but turned away again. "I agreed to my mother's request because . . ." Her voice dropped to the veriest whisper. "Because . . . I love you."

Daniel gave a shout of laughter that startled his wife before he moved to the bed and wrapped his arms around her. "Oh, my bonny Kate! My wonderful wife!"

"You—you do not mind?" Katherine asked, muffled against him.

He pulled back enough to look into her face. "Mind? No, I do not mind, my love." His lips covered hers, and Katherine gave herself up to his kiss. When he released her, she lay against his shoulder, thinking that perhaps she could bear his loving someone else if he would only kiss her as he just had.

"Katherine?" Daniel whispered.

"Yes?"

"Katherine, do you still want to know the woman who has stolen my heart? Who stole my heart the first time I saw her and has never relinquished it? Will always have my heart?"

She buried her face against his chest. She was wrong. She could not bear to hear him say such things about someone else. She shook her head.

He chuckled as her hair tickled his chin. Lifting her face to his, he smiled tenderly. "My darling Katherine, the woman who stole my heart has golden blond curls, beautiful blue eyes, and the most adorable dimples. She fits perfectly in my arms and has the most courageous heart in the world." He paused to place a kiss on Katherine's rounded lips before asking, "Do you know this incomparable?"

"Me? Oh, Daniel, is it me?"

"Of course it is you, my love."

"Oh, Daniel!" Katherine cried as she threw her arms around his neck. A sob broke from her, and she buried her face in his neck.

"Here, my love, don't cry. I hoped I would make you happy!"

"Oh, you did, Daniel, you did. From the first time you saw me?"

"From the very first. Before we left Mr. Muncie's best parlor, I was determined to marry you."

Katherine looked up at him. "When—when you stayed with me, you loved me then?"

"Yes, my sweet, I loved you then."

"I loved you, Daniel. I wanted to tell you then, but I thought you loved someone else. I didn't want to carry your child to ensure the estate but because if I were to lose you"—she paused to hug him close—"your child would be my only reason to live."

He kissed her before asking with a smile, "Is that the end of your foolish questions?"

Katherine surprised him again by saying, "No. It is not. I want to know who gave you that sapphire pin."

His laughter warmed her heart. "Ah? Were you jealous, my Kate?" At her nod, he hugged her as he whispered in her ear, "My mother gave me that jewel, my sweet, so you have no need to be concerned."

He held her against him, cradled to his chest, and his lips moved on hers. Katherine gave herself completely to him, holding back nothing.

Breathing deeply, Daniel raised his lips from hers and said, "If we are to eat our food before it spoils, we must discontinue this activity, Katherine."

"Daniel," Katherine said thoughtfully, "I have decided to always be honest from this day forward. And . . ." She paused to smile at her husband. "I need you more than food itself."

Daniel spoke no words, but the food grew cold on the trays.